Season of Fate

John Francis

FORWARD

After completing my first novel *Adventures from the ICPA: A Series of Short Stories* and a novelette titled *Between Realities: Stories of Liminality,* I realized how much I enjoyed writing in my free time. There were plenty of manuscripts I had never finished scattered about in the files on my computer, but one thing was certain: I seemed to do best writing short stories and not longer works.

I decided it was time to write something longer, and I had yet to write a novella. As for length a novella felt perfect as it was not as daunting as a long novel but would be more challenging than a novelette. Of course, there are varying definitions of what constitutes each length and type of work, but I was aiming for around twenty thousand words.

When puzzling out what kind of story would be best for a novella, I came to the realization that I had never written fantasy before. All of my previous works, and most of my uncompleted manuscripts, were simply realistic fiction. Fantasy worked well since I often get writer's block while writing long realistic fiction manuscripts. Writing fantasy was different. Having to build a world from scratch with its own rules, conventions, culture, and society was fascinating and kept me writing.

One fun aspect of this story is majority of it was written while it was snowing. Every time it snowed it would remind me of this manuscript and the Winter Kingdom I had constructed in my mind. I have always loved the winter and writing this story was the perfect thing to do with a cup of tea on a cold winter day, watching the snowflakes flutter down outside.

This was also my first time incorporating romance into a story. It was a challenge, and my beta readers really pushed me to improve the story from where it started. That being said, a special thanks to Sarah Mae, my primary beta reader who worked with this story from beginning to end, Isabel, my editor, and all of my other wonderful beta readers. Lastly, a big thanks to my mother, who listened to me read this story time and time again while offering feedback.

I hope readers can find comfort and confidence in the journey the characters take in self-discovery.

To anyone recovering from a toxic relationship, this story is for you. I hope it brings you healing.

The wind howled through the trees and flakes of snow blew against the windows, creating a hissing sound as the flames in the fireplace wavered with the gusts. It wasn't often we came to visit my grandmother while I was on break from university. She lived far from the city in the mountains, and even then, her cabin was nestled up away from the main town.

I wrapped myself tighter in the quilt I had been lent while I was visiting. I could hear light clattering sounds coming from the kitchen as my grandmother finished cleaning up after our evening meal. The rest of my family had headed back down the mountain to spend the night in a modern hotel with more space, but there was something I loved about spending time in my grandmother's cabin, so I had stayed behind.

The cabin was old, but not in a scary way. It was like a beautiful antique, cherished for all the years it had been around. I surveyed the living room. The velvety purple sectional sagged a bit and was piled with cream-colored pillows of different textures and sizes. In the picture window sat some small plants of a variety I didn't know, but they were comfortable with the cold and now had beautiful red berries. A slanted shelf opposite the window was cluttered with various crystals, and a black wood stove sat next to the shelf. It had a pot of glogg on top that filled the space with aromatics of spice and citrus. The whole eclectic space was tied together with a small chandelier that was quite out of place, yet still felt oddly right.

"Some weather we're having. Rin becomes more cold-hearted every year," my grandmother said as she entered the living room.

"Rin?"

"Yes, the snow prince. The reason winters are so violent and stormy in these parts."

That was one thing I loved about my grandmother. She had wonderful stories about the mountains in which she lived. I never knew if she just made them up herself to entertain me or if there was some semblance of truth in them. Whatever the case, I had many memories of being huddled up in the living room in which I currently sat, listening to all of her wonderful tales.

"Ah, yes, Rin the Snow Prince from the Winter Kingdom," my grandmother went on. "In these mountains a kingdom exists for each season. Each has its own rulers, laws, and traditions."

"Why is Rin so cold-hearted?"

"You better get comfortable, this story is a little bit of a long one," my grandmother said, giving me a playful wink.

I slid over and laid my head on her shoulder as she began to tell the tale.

"In the Svlavian mountains after a great battle long ago harmony was achieved between all the kingdoms. This meant that the Svlavlian people were blessed with warm temperate summers that never got too hot with just the right amount of rain to make the crops grow in abundance. The falls were crisp and cool with vibrant red and gold leaves that fluttered around in the breeze. Winters were snowy and pristine, but never bitterly cold. Springs came dressed in beautiful cherry and plum blossoms that clouded the mountainsides in various shades of pink. This harmony remained for many years, until one fateful event changed everything.

In the Winter Kingdom a prince was born, the queen named him Rin. He grew to be strikingly handsome. He was tall and thin with angular features and beautiful fine black hair. He was a very kind ruler and brought the beautiful snowy days where it's warm enough to walk outside and enjoy the flakes drifting through the air as well as stunning frost covered trees."

"What happened to him?" I asked, picturing the handsome prince in my mind.

"To get a better idea of Rin's fate I think we should take a deeper look," said my grandmother. She had one of those mischievous expressions she would get right before something magical happened. Every time she would tell a story, I would end up being transported into the storyline as a spectator. The living room would fade and give way to some other setting and the characters of the story would be there in front of me. One could argue I just had a great imagination, but it was as if I were actually there. I had never told my family about the strange occurrences that had taken place at my grandmother's cabin over the years; they were a little secret between my grandmother and me.

"Here, hold this," said my grandmother, handing me one of the crystals off the shelf. It was a light purple. It was such a light purple that it almost looked white. The way the crystals were arranged were reminiscent of snowflakes piled up.

I took the crystal and cradled it in the palms of my hands. The wind grew louder and shook the room around us to a frightening degree. The flames in the fireplace winked out and I felt the sting of snow on my face. Armchairs morphed into ice sculptures, door frames stretched into ornate archways, and the faint light from the kitchen transformed into a beautiful sunrise. The morning light poured in through a door to a balcony, and on the balcony stood the most handsome man I had ever seen. It had to be Rin.

It was official. He would become king the next winter season. Rin sat pondering this as he gazed over the Winter Kingdom. He was in line to ascend the throne after his mother retired, as was the kingdom's tradition. While he was ready, there was a lot on his mind. He turned upon hearing a set of light footsteps. Juniper, his head handmaiden, and only true friend, appeared. She was narrow framed with long blonde hair that was braided with native ice flowers and berries woven into the strands.

"You're at it again. Gazing wistfully over the horizon," she teased.

"I have been preparing my whole life for this moment. The people have spoken and are ready for me to be their leader, but I don't know if I have what it takes to rule like my mother. She has kept peace in the kingdom longer than any other ruler, the subjects trust her, and she spends so much of her time in the community I rarely even see her at the palace."

"I am sure with time you will be just like her, perhaps even better."

Rin knew Juniper meant well, but recently her words didn't really cheer him up that much. He had too much on his mind for simple encouragement to help. The pair walked to the throne room from the balcony. The Winter Palace was a sight to behold. Made of ice, it glistened in the sunlight during the day and sparkled at night under the stars. The throne room was made of frost covered trees planted in rows. Their branches spiraled upward and intertwined creating a sort of hallway to the throne.

The trees bared small red berries but were bereft of any leaves. At the end of the natural hallway was the throne itself. Also made of ice, it glowed a beautiful aquamarine. On the throne sat Rin's mother Anseia. It was easy to see where Rin got his looks as she was also stunningly beautiful. Her long blonde hair came down to her waist. Her skin was like porcelain, and her piercing violet eyes were mesmerizing, but calm.

"Rin, I am glad you're here. It's time for the sprites to read your future," said Anseia.

In the kingdoms the sprites were the one being that tied everyone together. Fortune tellers and magic wielders, the sprites were often called upon for guidance by the royal families. Anseia ushered Rin and Juniper to a secluded part of the palace. There in a dark thicket of trees the sprites had gathered. Small glowing beings, they floated in the cold winter air whispering to each other. Rin gazed at them in awe with a slight bit of fear. He had never seen the sprites before, only heard of them. They were like whisps of light dancing in the air against the inky backdrop of the space.

"All knowing sprites, Rin is here for guidance," said Anseia.

The sprites halted their murmurs as Rin entered into their circle. Then, they danced around as they chanted. After their ritual the leader among them spoke.

"Rin has a great challenge ahead of him. He will be tempted by warmth throughout his life."

The sprites then vanished after the cryptic message leaving Rin, Anseia, and Juniper alone in the dark thicket of trees. Rin took a deep breath. He sensed he would need much more than Juniper and his mother's support as he began to rule. His confidence wavered as he stood in the cold thicket of trees.

MIKAEL – THE RULES

I opened my eyes to find myself still in the living room. It seemed as though only minutes had passed, and I hadn't moved at all. I was elated to have experienced another one of my grandmother's magical stories. I wanted to know more.

"What did the sprites mean about Rin being tempted by warmth?" I asked.

"In the kingdoms, relationships are only possible between seasons that overlap. For example, those in the Winter Kingdom can only marry among themselves or with someone from the Fall or Spring Kingdoms. Falling in love with someone from the Summer Kingdom would be disastrous."

"Was there a reason for the rule? Why couldn't people love anyone from any kingdom?"

"Well, if someone were to fall in love with someone else from the opposite season, natural disasters could happen. Think of summer and winter. Heat melts ice. Falling in love could mean death. Natural disasters were not the only worry though. The lovers' hearts could possibly freeze or melt as well. Seasons directly connecting, like fall and winter, were safe from such misfortune."

I thought about how many taboo love stories there were throughout history. There had to be something similar among the kingdoms. "Had anyone ever fallen in love with someone from their opposite kingdom?" I asked.

"Of course, it happened with commoners from time to time. Those stories usually ended in tragedy like small floods, or forest fires, but it had never happened with royalty before. What Rin didn't know is that at the same time he was born, another prince was born in the Summer Kingdom. His name was Aarush. He was bursting with passion from his birth and grew to be a strong leader aside his father. Here, take this," my grandmother swapped out the crystal I was holding for a different one. This time the crystal was large and oblong. It appeared to be quartz. The next thing I knew I was no longer cold; it was summer.

Aarush sat on the throne next to his father Inigo. Aarush was tall and broad shouldered with short light brown hair. A work of pure muscle, he was physically capable of almost any task and was so strong he had started hunting with his father earlier than any other nobility ever had in the past. Aarush was free spirited and often aggressive which had gotten him into trouble multiple times as he worked to ascend to the throne since he often charged headfirst into any situation without considering consequences.

"Let's go hunting," Aarush said to his father with a pleading look. Despite his bulky stature and intense personality, he knew how to charm and talk his way into or out of just about anything.

"Hunting is a reward for when a day's work is done. There's still much left to do before then," came his father's reply.

"None of our work is going anywhere, please? We can make it quick. It doesn't have to be a long trip."

Inigo sighed, knowing that Aarush would keep up his pestering until they went. He himself was also fond of hunting, so he was easy to convince. "Fine, we can go, but we must be back before dusk to meet the sprites."

Aarush leapt up and ran off to the stables where they housed the phoenixes. Upon entering the stable, Aarush looked up at the beautiful bird in front of him. Signo was his personal phoenix and also his friend. They had gone hunting together ever since he was a boy. Mounting a saddle on Signo they flew into the air. Inigo followed close behind on his own phoenix.

The four soared higher and higher toward the sun until the blinding light encompassed them. When his eyes adjusted Aarush could see the surface of the sun just below with its heat waves and fire. He was attracted to the power of the sun - something so grand and bold that it affected every season.

As Signo swooped down toward the fiery orb, they could see small glowing fish jumping in and out of the sun's molten surface. Aarush deftly pulled out a net as they skimmed across the simmering plane and scooped up one of the fish. It wriggled in his net and sparks flew in all directions off its fins.

"Nice catch," called Inigo from behind.

Aarush waved in triumph to his father. The two of them, along with the phoenixes, twirled about above the flaming surface of the sun for a few more hours before making their decent back to the realm of the kingdoms. As they descended, all the seasons could be seen from above. The summer kingdom appeared green with mountaintops covered in a light mist. Fall was clear and one could see the many red, gold, and orange trees dotting the landscape. Spring was full of flowers of all colors, and winter was a solid white, and for the first time Aarush considered the mysteriousness of the kingdom compared to the others. He had seen it many times before, but there was something alluring about the mystery of the opposite realm. It was as if there was a magnet inside of him that pulled him closer to it.

"Father, why isn't it possible to see anything in the Winter Kingdom?"

"The snowstorms are too strong to see anything from this high, thus the Winter Kingdom is forever shrouded in a veil of snow. Despite never having visited, I do have some gifts from the Snow Queen Anseia from a meeting we had in the central point of where the kingdoms converge. I can show you after we get done talking with the sprites."

Aarush was excited to see something that had come from the kingdom of another season for the first time, so he patted Signo on the side and they sped up and landed quickly.

"Can I see the gift?" Aarush asked, shifting his weight between his feet, full of impatience.

"As I said, after meeting with the sprites."

Aarush was not happy about having to wait and his frustration bubbled a bit just like the solar flares that sometimes escaped from the sun. He decided to put his feelings aside since meeting with the sprites also seemed interesting enough.

The palace for the summer kingdom was not quite as exquisite as the Winter Kingdom. In fact, it was much more of a castle than a palace. Tall brick walls surrounded the edifice perched higher on a hill. It was always guarded even though any conflict between the kingdoms was so far in the past that no one even recalled it. Unlike the Winter Kingdom's palace, the castle was man-made and not as integrated into the nature itself.

Aarush and Inigo made their way to a secluded part of the castle where the glowing sprites were waiting in a small room. Just like with Rin, Aarush was guided to the center of their circle, and they danced about while reading the future.

"Aarush, you possess great passion. While it often brings you strength, that same passion is your weakness and through it you will end up hurting others." With another cryptic message, the sprites vanished.

"Father, what do they mean?" Aarush asked.

"The sprites never give direct answers, my son. They do make a point though; your passion is strong and fiery like the sun. That can be a good and bad thing. You must learn to control it not only for the sake of others, but also yourself."

The frustration was back for Aarush. All his life people had been telling him he was too brash, impatient, and selfish. These were not the qualities of a king and had hindered his progress toward the throne. Thankfully, he was able to calm himself by redirecting his attention to the gift his father had mentioned earlier. Inigo nodded and smiled leading them to a part of the castle that was even more secluded. Inside a dark room Inigo opened a large wooden cabinet with a key. Inside there were various treasures and gifts from other kingdoms that Aarush had never seen before. Pulling out a box embossed with a snowflake, Inigo handed the parcel to Aarush.

Aarush opened the box to find a small snipping from a tree with dark green leaves and red berries. The inside of the box was covered in frost and when he removed the branch from its housing, he noticed flakes of snow fall from it onto the ground.

"That, my son, is a branch from the royal throne room in the Winter Palace. The branches create snow and ice even here in the Summer Kingdom, but you must be careful. Heat and cold don't mix well. If these gifts are not returned to their boxes Winter Kingdom magic could escape and bring snow, cold, or worse to our kingdom. Make sure to always put the branch back into the box. The gifts here must remain under lock and key for everyone's safety."

Aarush was enamored by the strange branch. After seeing it, something inside him stirred. The branch was like a small window into a world he had never seen before. He wanted to open that window wider, see more…feel more. That night after everyone had gone to sleep, he silently slipped back over to the secluded area of the castle. Entering the room, only the moonlight poured through the window. He didn't dare light a candle for fear of alerting the palace guards.

Opening the large cabinet carefully as to not let the heavy wooden doors squeak, he looked at all the boxes, each with an emblem matching the season from which the gift was given. He scanned the boxes until he found the one from earlier and immediately pulled it off the shelf to take another look at the branch, after admiring it sparkling in the moonlight his curiosity mounted and he pulled out every box he could find with a snowflake. While he had visited both the fall and spring kingdoms due to their overlap, the Winter Kingdom was shrouded in mystery.

In the other boxes Aarush found many interesting artifacts that gave him a better idea of what the Winter Kingdom was hiding. One box had a glistening frozen fruit, and upon opening another, a cold wind blew out and snowflakes danced around in the air. Aarush pulled his sleeves down, unused to the cold. These artifacts were magical and piqued Aarush's interest even more.

Hearing footsteps in the hall he quickly closed the boxes and returned them to the cabinet locking it just in time for the guards to enter the room. He hid around the corner of a pillar controlling his breathing as to not be noticed.

After returning to his quarters, he pondered the recent developments. The more he learned about the Winter Kingdom the more he wanted to see it, but at the same time it presented grave dangers and challenges. What would happen if his father found out? What would his subjects think if they found out? Being the only heir to the throne and rarely being told "no" made these thoughts less of a hindrance. Aarush brashly pushed aside these concerns, and in his usual fashion decided to go forward without fully considering the consequences. His mind was made up. He would visit the Winter Kingdom secretly to see it for himself.

RIN - AS PATHS CROSS

Rin sat hunkered into a pile of pillows on his bed gazing out over the snowy mountains. His quarters were in one of the uppermost spires of the palace, one of the safest places. The interior was cloaked in various hues of pink, purple, and blue that blended with the winter sky that could be clearly seen out the large windows. Juniper and his mother both sat in ornate chairs near his bed.

"What did they mean? Tempted by warmth?" Rin was very uneasy hearing this kind of fortune right before taking the throne. Now he had to not only focus on being a strong ruler, but simultaneously stay strong against an elusive threat.

"You are drawn to the opposite kingdom. The Summer Kingdom. A place you can never visit," replied Anseia.

The gears turned in Rin's mind. He never had any interest in the Summer Kingdom and being forbidden to visit never bothered him. He was well aware of the consequences.

"I have to attend to the royal court. Juniper will keep you company I'm sure," said Anseia gracefully gliding out of the room, her iridescent cape billowing behind her.

After she was well out of earshot Juniper piped up. "There has to be more to this than your mother is letting on. Think about it. In all of the other kingdoms the royalty meet every year on the summer and winter solstice in the core, the center of where our kingdoms connect, but you have never been allowed to go. With this most recent fortune and her reaction I think your mother is keeping you from something…or something from you."

Anseia, had far more information from the sprites due to their visit at Rin's birth. At that time, they spoke to her of another prince, born in the Summer Kingdom on the very same day who would be very dangerous to Rin. Anseia had done everything in her power, including giving many gifts to the Summer Kingdom to keep the peace and also keep Rin from ever discovering the other prince, Aarush.

As much as Rin didn't like the thought of his mother keeping secrets from him, he was beginning to agree with Juniper more and more as the years went by. He also knew that if his mother wouldn't share the truth, there was another way.

"To get a better idea of what is going on I think we should visit a sorceress in the mountains."

Juniper was clearly taken aback by this request from the expression on her face. In the Winter Kingdom's mountains lived the sorceresses. They had a delicate relationship with the rest of the kingdom. In the distant past the kingdom was split into smaller states, some run by sorceresses and some by the current royal family. This caused many clashes until a final battle had resulted in unification under the royal family. Now, the royalty left the sorceresses alone so that they wouldn't cause any trouble and so it had remained for many years, at least according to the average person. However, in some of the town bars late at night one could catch murmurs of stories of people visiting the sorceresses for help with magic and the supernatural.

"Can't you just live with your fortune from the sprites? What more can a sorceress offer?" Juniper asked.

"Not really, it ended up causing more questions than answers. I don't need to go get some magic spell from a sorceress, but I do know that they have a library. It is full of ancient lore, and perhaps we can find a bit more about what the sprites are hinting at."

"You always were one to study too much," Juniper forced out a small laugh, clearly trying and failing to lighten the mood.

That very moment, Rin jumped up. "We need to get to the reindeer stable."

Juniper had worried that Rin would be unstoppable once he got his mind on the idea of visiting the sorceresses, and as she feared, she was right.

Aarush was fidgety all day. The only thing he could think about were all of the beautiful and mysterious items he found inside the cabinet. They were like small pieces of a puzzle he had not completed. The branch made him wonder what the full throne looked like. The fruit made him want to see an entire tree filled with them. When his father offered to go hunting Aarush quickly turned down the offer.

"Are you feeling alright?" asked Inigo.

"Yeah, I'm fine, but just really tired today for some reason. I think I should rest," Aarush replied, hoping to get a moment alone to slip back to see the gifts again.

"Alright, do visit the royal doctor though. I don't want you getting sick at a time like this. The transition of power and you taking the throne is already almost too much to handle."

After reassuring his father and seeing him fly off on a phoenix into the sun, Aarush dashed back to the secluded room to get another look at the treasures within. As he pushed the doors open, he immediately knew something was off. The air was cold and caused the hair on his arms and legs to stand on end. He let out a small shiver. Pushing aside the curtain he stood in shock.

He had forgotten to put away a single box in his haste the night before. An open box with one of the beautiful branches sat on a side table near the cabinet. Snowflakes floated upward out of the box into the air before fluttering back down, glinting in the light as they descended. Frost had completely covered the room, including the glass on the window making it refract the light through the crystals in another dazzling display.

Quickly closing the box and returning it, Aarush then hastily opened the window letting in the hot summer air. The frost evaporated into mist almost instantly. He let out a sigh of relief. It would be risky to keep coming back to study the items housed in the castle. If his father found out, his chances of visiting the Winter Kingdom would become even less likely. There had to be another way.

Aarush decided that he would have to do something he usually hated...study. Before he knew it his feet had guided him to the palace library. The room was located on the top floor in the center of the castle and had arched windows all the way around. Mahogany bookcases were carved with intricate designs and held books from throughout the ages. It smelled a bit musty from all the old paper. The palace historian, Edna, oversaw the catalogue of books. She not only maintained the library, but also reviewed new books from scholars around the kingdom and deemed which ones were worthy enough to be added to the collection. With her vast knowledge she had also been Aarush's teacher when he was younger.

"Aarush, what brings you to the library?" asked Edna. It was clear she was slightly suspicious as she narrowed her eyes. She had been responsible for Aarush's schooling and the library was somewhere he had avoided most of his life.

"Since I am going to be crowned king in the near future, I realized I need to study each of the kingdoms so that I can be a better ruler," he lied.

"I see you have matured with age," smiled Edna. "Now let's see, what do we have on the kingdoms." Edna led Aarush through the massive bookcases to a particular section of especially old looking books. "These should do," she said, pulling a stack from one of the shelves. One for each season.

The books had leather covers each in a different faded color. A dusty pink for spring, green for summer, pumpkin for fall, and an icy blue for winter. Aarush sat at one of the tables and immediately snatched up the blue book. If he had been paying more attention, he would have seen a knowing smirk cross Edna's face.

"Are you sure this is a good idea?" cautioned Juniper. She and Rin were in the palace stable putting on their coats and scarves to prepare for the trek to the mountains by sleigh. Rin's coat was an iridescent lavender with puffy white fur around the collar and cuffs. It had gold buttons as a finishing touch. Juniper's coat was less extravagant but still warm. It was woven from a sky-blue thread and had short grey fur edging.

Joining the two on the journey was Zeb a white reindeer with brown fuzzy antlers. He was one of the only reindeer the stable hands wouldn't notice missing since he was still young and not fully trained. Zeb and Juniper got along well as Juniper had learned the language of reindeer and could communicate with them, so having her along for the trip would hopefully help things go smoothly.

"I won't be able to continue on as the leader of our great nation if I don't know why things are the way they are. First, I am called to be our next ruler and then the next thing I know I am being cautioned about a vague looming danger I can't comprehend. How can I lead effectively with that constantly hanging over my head?"

Seeing no argument that could stand up against Rin's sound reasoning Juniper hopped up into the sleigh and took the reins. With a snap they were off as Zeb galloped gleefully over the snow. Soon they were on a narrow path winding through thick fir trees that were hunched over with the weight of snow on their branches. It was nearing dusk, and the sky was painted with fiery strokes of pink and orange on an indigo canvas.

As the sun continued to set, they made their way deeper into the forest. There were a few lanterns lit along the side of the road at first, but the further they ventured the lanterns gave way to small stone pillars on the side of the path as guidance. Eventually even these stone beacons disappeared and the only way to tell they were on course was to follow ribbons tied on trunks of trees.

"How much further, Zeb?" yelled Juniper. He snorted and huffed in reply. "He says it will be a bit longer before we get there. Try to be patient."

"Why are you asking me to be patient?" Rin asked, turning to Juniper.

"Your feet have been pressed up against the dash this whole time as if that would make us go faster." She laughed.

"I guess you are right," said Rin sheepishly realizing he had been subconsciously forcing his weight against the sleigh. "Do you think they will have the answers we seek?"

"I can't guarantee anything, but for your sake, I hope they do."

The trio plodded along for a while until they were nearing the tops of the mountains. The sky had darkened and snow with big fluffy flakes began to whirl around them. Rin pulled his cloak over his head. The squall became worse and worse to the point that even with a lantern it was almost impossible to see where they were going.

"Do you think we should stop here and wait for the storm to pass?" asked Juniper.

While Rin wanted to press on the wind was strong and icy. He was about to agree when he noticed some strange lights up ahead. "I think we have actually reached our destination just in time."

Zeb pulled the sleigh closer and the three of them ducked out of the snow thanks to an icy overhang. Under the overhang was a small cave with a pink flickering lantern. They gazed at it in awe. Never before had they encountered pink fire. This was for sure the home of one of the sorceresses. The two travelers exchanged a nervous glance. Inside the cave was a heavy wooden door with a brass knocker. Clanking the metal against the wood door, Rin prayed that someone was home.

"Come in," trilled a voice as the door creaked open.

Rin and Juniper entered, leaving Zeb with the sleigh. Inside was a small alcove made of ice. On the walls hung tapestries in vibrant colors depicting scenes from the Winter Kingdom. A cauldron sat in the center of the room and bubbled a strange blue, fluorescent mixture that illuminated the rest of the space.

"I am Prince Rin, of the Royal Family, and this is my handmaiden, Juniper," said Rin.

"I knew you were coming," replied the sorceress. She had similar looks to Rin, narrow and angular in stature with long white hair. She wore a pale pink dress that was embroidered with white flowers. On her head a sort of ice berry crown was perched. While she had a softer appearance, one could see in her eyes that she answered to no one.

She motioned for the two to sit near the cauldron on some chairs covered in animal hides. Rin and Juniper obliged and nervously eyed the bubbling concoction.

"I've heard there is a library somewhere in the mountains with ancient lore. The sprites told me I will always be drawn to the warmth. I want to know what that means and how I can combat this threat that remains in a mysterious shadow."

"Rin, dear. Books don't have all the answers. I think you know as well as I do that you didn't come here to seek out some old, tattered pages. You came for a fortune telling." Juniper looked to Rin hoping he would back out, but one look at his expression told her he was set on going through with his plan. "You came to the right place. The sprites think they hold all the power convincing the royal families to trust them with their future, but they neglect to say there are other ways to get a more accurate fortune."

"What do you mean by 'more accurate ways?'" asked Juniper suspiciously.

"A wise handmaiden you have," smirked the sorceress revealing a set of small fangs. "Nothing in the universe is free. You give me something and I can give you something in return. An even trade."

Rin pulled out a crystal, unphased by the sorceress. It was a light purple, such a light purple that it almost looked white. The arrangement of the crystal structure looked like little snowflakes piled up.

"Rin, you can't just go giving away one of the royal crystals for a fortune," protested Juniper.

"Ahhh, I can tell you are willing to make a great sacrifice to learn of your future. With this trade I can give you a very detailed fortune," said the sorceress, eyeing the crystal.

Rin started to hand over the crystal when his hands froze. This was a precious family heirloom. Giving it away was betraying his mother. The consequences could be severe. At the same time, without some kind of drastic choice, how was he going to find out anything about his fate with everyone being so secretive and cryptic. Had he been informed years ago he could have approached things with more caution, but he felt as though time had already run out.

"I have made up my mind. If I don't make this sacrifice, I have no idea how severe the threat to me may be, and no way of preventing it. Here take it," said Rin, passing the crystal to the sorceress.

She dropped it into the cauldron and the color of the light changed to a light purple similar to the crystal itself. Then reaching into the bubbling brew she withdrew a shining orb. Inside were images that passed too fast for Rin and Juniper to catch, but the sorceress stared at them intently.

"As I expected, almost everything comes down to love. You will fall in love with someone warm, no, fiery and passionate. A warrior. This love could be your greatest strength or your greatest downfall depending on how you choose to proceed." The room then went completely black for a moment before the original color of the cauldron re-illuminated.

Rin sat puzzled. The description of the person he would fall in love with was nothing like he had imagined. A warrior? Being a pacifist himself, he was confused by the notion.

"How are we going to explain this to your mother?" Juniper broke the silence, clearly worried about the crystal.

"My young naïve friends, there is much more to the Winter Kingdom than you know. Rin, by coming here you have already proven that you are a stronger ruler than you realize. As a token of my appreciation, take this pendant. If your mother protests your coming here, simply give her this and it will remedy everything."

Rin took the pendant and looked at it carefully. It looked like granite, but it was composed of flecks of deep indigo, teal, and rose. Engraved into the pendant was a symbol he didn't recognize. It looked something like a fan or a clamshell.

"Thank you for your hospitality and service, we shall be going now," Rin announced. The sorceress guided them to the door. "Also, I never got your name."

"Symensia."

After divulging this piece of information, the sorceresses guided Rin and Juniper back out of the cave to where Zeb was waiting.

"Safe travels back to the palace, and remember I am here if you need anything else." Symensia smiled again revealing her fangs, but this time she seemed far less threatening.

"Thank you," said Rin bowing as Juniper curtsied next to him. "We will be on our way now."

Having eaten a bit of hay outside while waiting, Zeb was already full of energy and eagerly pranced about as Rin hitched him back to the sleigh. In no time, they were speeding back down the mountain.

Aarush poured over the history of the Winter Kingdom looking for anything that could be of use. He was intrigued to find that the kingdom had not always been shrouded in thick clouds blocking out the view from above. This appeared to have something to do with a secretive agreement between the royal family and sorceresses. Ever since this event, which the book didn't detail, the Winter Kingdom had become much more closed off.

"You seem to have an interest in the Winter Kingdom," said Edna, sliding another book onto the table. "This one is more recent. It was written just last year and gifted to us due to some diplomatic relations."

Aarush nodded and opened it. There on the page was a man about the same age as him. He had short dark hair and everything about him was sharp. His jawline was especially strong and angular, and he had beautiful violet eyes. The mysterious person wore indigo robes, and in his hands, he held…the branch from the closet.

"Edna, who is this?" Aarush asked holding up the book.

"Did you retain anything I taught you in school? The caption clearly says he is the current prince of the Winter Kingdom. Rin."

There was something alluring about Rin. He was another part of the mystery. He wasn't just handsome. There was depth to him. Even from the pictures Aarush could tell that there was an aura about Rin that made him seem emotionally strong, intelligent, and reasonable, qualities Aarush himself lacked. Also, this beautiful prince somehow had a connection to the branch gifted to the Summer Kingdom. He wanted to ask Edna about the branch, but he couldn't figure out a way to bring it up without raising suspicion. Instead, he asked perhaps an even more risky question without thinking.

"Is there a way for royalty to cross between forbidden kingdoms?"

Edna raised an eyebrow but obliged in answering the question. "The laws of this realm dictate that opposite seasons cannot intermingle, but I would be lying if I said royalty had never crossed between the kingdoms. I happen to know a story of that exact situation."

Aarush waited expectantly as Edna began.

"Many years ago, the Winter Kingdom had two Princesses, Symensia and Anseia. The current queen, as you know, is Anseia because she was always the more level-headed of the two. Symensia was never happy with her life in the Winter Kingdom and ended up falling for one of the nobles in the Summer Kingdom. She crossed over many times, but things ended tragically and now she and her daughter live apart in separate seasons and her lover… he didn't make it."

"What do you mean by that?"

34

"If two royals fall in love across opposite seasons, one of the elements always wins over the other. In the case of winter and summer either the heart of the summer person will freeze, or the heart of the winter person will melt. Commoners don't have strong enough associations with the season to cause death, but a royal affair is different."

Considering this Aarush glanced over the picture of Rin again. He knew he had to meet Rin. There was something alluring about him, but there was also something that needed to be solved, some sort of loose ends that needed to be tied up. The more he searched the less clear things became. He was, however, gaining more pieces to the puzzle.

When Edna went back to organizing books at her desk Aarush slipped over to the part of the library containing books for spells, potions, and the like. He knew somewhere in the midst of them had to be the instructions on how to find his way across the seasons to the Winter Kingdom.

Rummaging through the books, he found one that was pushed behind the others. It was small and had the emblem for each season pressed into the leather cover. Inside the cover was a handwritten note. *Keep this safe. If you ever need to see me, it will help you. – Symensia*

Aarush was surprised to find a note from Symensia herself, the very person from Edna's story. Flipping through the pages, he came upon what he was looking for. A crudely drawn map of the four kingdoms and notes on traversing between them. The book certainly wasn't a published manuscript and appeared almost like a personal research journal. He pocketed the book and returned to the main table. Edna was too busy to notice.

After a few more hours of looking through the book on the Winter Kingdom, he decided it was time to depart before raising any more suspicion than he already had.

"I am headed out."

"Take those books on the Winter Kingdom with you. Looks like you have a lot of studying to do," said Edna with a wink.

Aarush nodded, scooping up the books. He felt strange as he carried them back to his quarters. Edna was far too calm about the situation. In fact, she was not just calm, she was helpful with all of his questions and even gave him a book with more information. Perhaps Edna knew he had the small journal. Had she put it there for him to find in the first place?

That night Aarush sprawled out on his bed with the various books in front of him. By candlelight he read as much as he could and took notes with a quill and ink. It appeared from the small book that it was possible to get to the Winter Kingdom by going through the core. It was a sacred center to all the seasonal kingdoms. Every year on the summer and winter solstice as well as the spring and fall equinox the leaders would all gather at this location. The only issue was the area was not simply open and clear. There were guards stationed to monitor and make sure no one slipped through.

Flipping through the other notes in the book, however, it appeared that it would be possible to get through by contacting Soldren, the headmaster of the core. He oversaw all of the inner workings of how the seasons fit together, and he was apparently fond of collecting rare specimens from each seasonal kingdom. By offering Soldren something he didn't have, he was happy to allow undeterred passage. The only question was, what did he not already have? It was time to find out.

Aarush made up his mind right then and there that he would go ask Soldren himself what kind of offering could provide him passage into the Winter Kingdom. On the next day his father went hunting alone Aarush prepared himself for the journey. He told the palace staff he would be studying hard that day and requested to not be disturbed. Packing a small bag, he set off toward the core of the kingdoms. With the help of Signo, he arrived in no time. The phoenix landed gracefully next to a heavy wooden door in the side of a mountain. Surrounding the door were stones that had been carefully placed together like a puzzle. It was warm out and stars dotted the evening sky overhead as evergreen trees ominously shadowed the duo as they stood.

Leaving Signo behind Aarush entered the door to find himself immediately exiting into a clearing surrounded by trees. The opening from which he exited in the new realm was a portal centered between two stone pillars. He now stood in a circle of four sets of pillars. Each set he assumed must lead to a different season, but none of the other portals were active.

The core was strange. It was all of the seasons and none of the seasons at once. Scraggly trees surrounded the clearing and bared autumn leaves; however, winter frost covered their surface. The grass was green as if it were summer and butterflies flitted about like spring. It was a disconcerting, yet oddly enthralling experience.

Aarush took a deep breath. He was getting closer and closer to finishing the puzzle. Hopefully Soldren had another piece for him.

It was nearly midnight as Zeb pulled Rin and Juniper back to the palace. Eyeing the windows, Rin was relieved to see that the candle in his mother's room was extinguished. Maybe they could have this whole escapade go unnoticed. The trio arrived back in the stable and got Zeb settled for the night. He was clearly proud of himself for getting his friends to and from the mountains. Rin poured him a small bowl of oats as a reward, and he happily chomped away as Juniper hung up their winterwear.

They then snuck back into the palace, Juniper to her quarters and Rin to his. He did however have to pass Anseia's room on his way up the spire. As he tiptoed by, suddenly the candles illuminated themselves and his mother stepped into the hall.

"Well, looks like someone's home. I know you went to see a sorceress in the mountains."
Rin froze, trying to read her expression.
"I know about the royal crystal too. Now that you have met a sorceress, I won't hide my own powers anymore."

Rin stood in shock. His own mother possessed magic abilities which explained the candles coming to life on their own.

"You have magi…" Rin started.

"Don't act shocked, I'm sure Symensia told you everything. Part of me is angry with you for going, but at the same time I'm angry at myself for hiding this from you."

"She didn't tell me anything other than my own fortune, well, and to give you this," said Rin pulling out the pendant.

Anseia froze. Her expression was somewhere between shock and bewilderment. Rin gently placed the pendant into her hand.

"There's something you must know..." Rin waited patiently as his mother recollected her feelings. "Symensia is my sister. I gave her this pendant when we parted ways."

He never knew his mother had any siblings. He had unknowingly visited his aunt for advice which made much more sense as to why she was grateful for his visit.

"Why did you never tell me?"

"I didn't want you to visit her and get a reading on your future. I've been trying all my life to protect you from the threat of warmth. At your birth the sprites warned me of the danger, so I did everything in my power to keep you away from the Summer Kingdom and the sorceresses in the mountains, but alas I failed you as a mother and broke your trust by keeping all of this from you."

"Mother, I have no interest in visiting the Summer Kingdom, in fact I went to learn more about the danger to my life so that I could be a better ruler and avoid the threat of the warmth," said Rin as he and Anseia sat down on a bench in the hallway.

"What worries me my love is that something inevitable will happen. No matter what I do to protect you." Rin rested his head on her shoulder, and she stroked his hair like when he was little. It helped him feel better despite the bleak realization.

"What would happen if I entered the Summer Kingdom?" asked Rin.

"Well, nothing would happen if you simply entered, but falling in love. That would be a disaster. In fact, that's what caused the rift between my sister and me. She fell in love with a noble from the Summer Kingdom and they secretly visited each other for many years. When they had a child one of the worst floods ravaged the mountains. It is our job to keep everyone safe. If something happened between you and another royal, I fear the damage would be more than we could recover from."

"Mother, I know you were trying to protect me, but I wish you would've told me this earlier, I could have prepared myself. I now know to be very wary of the Summer Kingdom. Do you think they have a motive to cause such destruction?"

Anseia pondered this for a moment. "I don't think they have ill intent. The kingdoms have been at peace for many years." She looked at a grandfather clock in the hallway. "You have had too much information today though. It's a lot to think about at once, how about you get some rest?"

Rin wasn't sure if he was, excited, angry, or simply confused at this point. So many emotions swirled around his head.

The two of them made their way up to Rin's quarters in the spire. His mother hadn't tucked him into bed for over ten years, but she did that night, pulling the covers up to his chin and sitting beside his bed. The only light came from a lone candle on the bedside table. They sat together for a moment in silence as the shadows danced about on the walls from the flickering flame.

"Rin, you are my greatest treasure. I can't bear to lose you. I almost lost my sister, and I can't go through something like that again."

"I understand. One last question. If you and Symensia both have powers, does that mean…"

"Yes, my son. You do too."

Rin looked down at his hands trying to comprehend what having magic meant. His head was spinning again. He gave up trying to process everything that had just happened as his mother extinguished the candle so they could both turn in for the night. One would have expected Rin to lay awake trying to take in all the new information he had been bombarded with, but rather after his head stopped spinning, these realizations provided a sort of peace. He was starting to understand why his life had been a certain way up until the present, and he felt that he was beginning to understand the threat he was up against. Maybe, with this newfound information he could protect himself and his kingdom.

Aarush's call was met with no reply, but there was a clear path into the forest that he decided to follow. The strange mix of seasons continued through the forest, and it felt both warm and cold at once. As he made his way down the path he came to a clearing and in the center was nestled a small cottage.

The abode had a thick straw roof, brick walls, and shuttered windows that were currently open. Flower baskets hung under each window, but there was something strange. Each basket housed plants from a different season.

Approaching the cottage, Aarush could see that there was a pie sitting on the windowsill to cool. The sweet aroma wafted over as he grew closer. The air around the cottage was calm and pleasant. Aarush knocked on the door hoping he could get directions to Soldren.

"Why, hello there," said an old man opening the door. He was dressed in a dark blue robe and had a long white beard. His posture was hunched, and he walked with a wooden cane. "I don't get many visitors here in the core, what brings you this direction?"

"I'm looking for Soldren."

The old man's eyes sparkled. "You've come to the right place. Come in and have a piece of pie. I just made it with berries from the Winter Kingdom."

Aarush eagerly entered the cottage with hopes of trying an actual food from the Winter Kingdom. As he passed through the doorway he took in the setting. It was fairly dark inside save for the natural light from the windows. All around the room were shelves and shelves of boxes just like those he had found in the castle. Each box had the emblem of a season on it.

"Wait, are you Soldren?" said Aarush in surprise. None of the books in the library had any pictures of the wizard.

"Yes, I am," the old man chuckled.

The two seated themselves at the kitchen table and Soldren cut a piece of the pie. It was perfectly balanced between sweet and tart. A flavor that Aarush had never tasted before. He wanted to ask for a second piece but calmed himself enough to ask the big question.

"Soldren, how do I visit the Winter Kingdom?"

"Ahhh, so it is illicit passage you seek."

"I just, I want to know more…" Aarush trailed off, unsure if Soldren would help him or just alert his father.

"Relax, I'll help you. As you can see, I am a bit of a collector," said Soldren motioning to all the boxes surrounding them. There were even some in the kitchen. "Find me something I don't have, and I will more than happily get you there."

"Is there anything you still need? I can't imagine there is much you don't have."

Aarush took another glance around the room. With so many compartments around the house it seemed as if Soldren had already completed his collection.

"I do have just about everything, but some things are consumable. In fact, after baking this pie I need more berries from the Winter Kingdom. Sadly, you are not from there, but…"

"I can get you a branch that has some," Aarush interrupted as he remembered the branch with the berries he had found.

"Really?" pondered Soldren, clearly impressed. "Bring it here and we can discuss your passage."

"Thank you, sir," said Aarush as he ran out the door and back to the portals. Jumping through the still open portal into the Summer Kingdom he mounted Signo and flew back to the castle. He had Signo land right outside of the window with the room that stored the gifts. He pried it open and hopped inside, only to come face to face with Inigo.

"Father?"

"What are you doing sneaking in here? The servants already told me they saw you come in here multiple times after I showed you the gift from the Winter Kingdom."

"I, uh, wanted to look at the gifts more. They were just so beautiful and exotic. I...couldn't help myself." What Aarush said was at least partly truthful. His stomach knotted up with nervous energy.

"That still doesn't explain why you went to such lengths as to sneak in the window."

"Just to be safe..."

"Also, what is the meaning of all of the books on the Winter Kingdom I found in your room?"

Now Aarush was trapped. His mind raced trying to think of a logical explanation. "I just wanted to know more," he managed.

"This is like Symensia all over again," grumbled Inigo.

"Symensia?" Aarush was surprised to hear his father bring up her name after he learned about her in his studies.

"Yes, she caused us enough trouble already. We don't need more problems between our two kingdoms."

"What happened?"

The next thing Aarush knew, he was seated in his father's study. Located on the north side of the castle it didn't get much light and the candles on the desk didn't seem to help either. Around them were shelves of books and ornate red velvet curtains with gold tassels hung around the windows.

"I am telling you this as a cautionary tale. You need to let go of your interest in the Winter Kingdom. It's a place you can never go. In the past, Symensia broke our sacred rules and crossed over to the Summer Kingdom. She met a baron and they fell in love and had a daughter. Edna."

Aarush's eyes widened. Edna was the daughter of a Summer Kingdom baron and Winter Kingdom princess. It would explain why she was so understanding and helpful about his curiosity.

"What's so bad about that? They loved each other enough to find a way to unite."

"But it caused great damage. Floods and pouring rain followed. It took us years to recover. Now Symensia and Edna must live forever apart too. In the end, all their love caused was heartache and loss."

"How are all of the Kingdoms supposed to work together if we can't even visit or see certain places?"

"As you know, every year the royalty goes to the core to meet. Once you become king you will go too. You can meet the Winter Kingdom royalty then, and perhaps, as with the branch, you will be gifted something as well." Inigo came around the desk to pat Aarush on the shoulder. "Here, I brought you something." Inigo pulled out the box.

Aarush knew right away it was the branch. "Thank you, father."

"Sorry to interrupt, but you have visitors in the throne room," said a palace advisor, peeking through the door.

Inigo departed, leaving Aarush alone. He opened the box and gazed at the beautiful branch with the winter berries. He was so conflicted. Part of him wanted to use this branch to visit the Winter Kingdom, but he didn't want to endanger anyone. However, unlike Symensia, he didn't have any love interest in the Winter Kingdom; he simply wanted to meet Rin and ask him questions.

What was it like always having cloud cover? How did they stay warm there? What new types of food could he try? How could they create better diplomatic relations between their kingdoms? As he thought about all his questions, he came to the conclusion that it wasn't really an issue since he was going on a little fact-finding mission, not on some romantic escapade. There was still a risk, however for Aarush, that risk was worth it.

While Rin certainly felt more prepared for what was to come, he still couldn't get all the newly discovered information off his mind. He was related to the sorceresses in the mountains and had unknowingly visited his aunt for help. After a light breakfast of oatmeal and winter berries, he called upon Zeb to get him down to the frozen lake near the palace. Whenever he was stressed, he would skate on the ice. From a young age he had been trained in figure skating as a recreational activity.

He slipped on his white and gold skates and glided out onto the ice as Zeb watched patiently from the sidelines. Rin twirled around the lake as the sun continued to rise dusting the snowscape in rosy light as if the realm were putting on blush to start the day. As he skated his mind centered in on the issue at hand.

With his newly found confidence, he decided it would be in his best interest to return to the mountains and once again seek out the help of his aunt and the other sorceresses to learn more about the threat to his life. He hoped Symensia would take him before the high council of sorceresses. The council was a group of the strongest magic wielders in the kingdom. They oversaw the sorceress's society high in the mountains. The society operated somewhat like a kingdom within the kingdom, although now sorceresses no longer had the power they used to. Perhaps they would have more answers for him.

Landing a triple axel perfectly, he let out a sigh of relief and made his way back over to Zeb. The reindeer sat enjoying a bowl of oats Rin had brought along as a treat and thank you. In an uncharacteristic move he decided to go back to the mountains alone rather than bringing along Juniper.

"Alright Zeb, you've had your treat. I'll give you another if you can take me back to the mountains," although he couldn't understand Zeb like Juniper could, he knew the answer was a yes.

Hopping up on the saddle the two galloped off up the mountain. Little did they know Anseia and Juniper had been watching Rin's skating performance from the palace terrace.

"Where do you think he and Zeb are off to?" asked Juniper.

"There is only one place he would be going without telling anyone. I am positive he will go back to seek the wisdom of the sorceresses."

"Do you have anything against him going?"

Anseia pondered this for a moment. "Not really, I would have in the past, but it seems the two of you were able to really connect with my sister Symensia when you went last time. Perhaps Rin's drive to find the truth will finally bring our kingdom together."

"You don't actually know what the threat is either," Juniper said after hearing Anseia's thoughts.

"You're right. As much as I have worked to protect Rin over the years, I don't know much more than the fact that the threat will come from the Summer Kingdom."

Juniper and Anseia then sat in silence sipping on cups of winter berry tea wondering what information Rin would bring back to share, and if he would even be willing to share what he discovered.

By the time Rin and Zeb had made progress up the mountain to Symensia's cave it was late afternoon.

"Ahh, you have returned. My reading wasn't enough for you?"

"Symensia, I was honored to receive your reading, but I know there has to be more. You said books don't have all the answers, but I am sure they can at least provide some direction. I beg you to take me to the high council of sorceresses and the collection of knowledge they possess."

"Rin, dear, I have no qualms about taking you to the high council, you simply had to show you were ready. You have grown a lot since I last saw you. I am pleased to hear that you understand the importance of our sacred library. Books don't provide answers, as you said they provide direction. They are like street signs that can point you down the right path. With this outlook you are certainly ready. Come, we must move quickly to reach the council before dusk."

Symensia and Rin attached a sled to Zeb, and he pulled them along a narrow path up the side of one of the nearby mountains. Rin wasn't sure, but it seemed Symensia's magic was the only thing keeping them from sliding off the narrow path and plummeting to their demise. The path was rocky and only wide enough for the sled. Zeb seemed unbothered and happily pulled the two of them along.

When they arrived at the very top of the mountain the cold wind whipped around everything, and Rin could feel the chill though his heavy cloak. There was a small lean-to with hay where Zeb went to rest. In the opposite direction was the mountain peak. A stone structure had been built into mountain itself and spiraled up around the peak. Windows were interspersed into the structure, and each had a single candle.

Upon entering, Rin and Symensia worked their way up the cold stone steps. Despite the candles there wasn't much light as the sun had started to set. The wind rattled the thin glass panes on the windows and the snow hissed as it brushed up against the glass. At the top of the staircase, they entered a room perched on the very top of the mountain with tall, thin windows on the walls. Mauve misty twilight was all that illuminated the space except for a fire in the fireplace. Pillows in varying shades of lavender were strewn about the corners of the room and sorceresses all lounged about chatting.

"Welcome, Rin," said the eldest, rising from the only chair in the room. "I am Vanslen, the head sorceress. We finally get to meet you in person. A momentous occasion seeing as you are half sorcerer yourself. While your mother closed herself off from us, you come to seek our help. A wise decision from our up-and-coming king. We will do whatever we can to help you as a demonstration of our gratitude."

Although his mother had always warned him of the dangerous sorceresses, Rin was beginning to feel that there was some sort of grave misunderstanding. The magic wielders he had met so far had all been kind, helpful, and immediately welcomed him.

"Thank you for your kindness. I hope to bridge the gap between our two communities going forward. We all live in the same kingdom and should have peace and a mutualistic relationship. I come requesting access to the library, as well as your guidance finding lore on the threat to my life."

"A wise one indeed," piped up one of the other sorceresses.

The group murmured amongst themselves and came to the conclusion that Rin could enter the library with Vanslen as his guide.

"With all decided it is time for us to turn in for the night. We shall delve deep into the lore tomorrow when we are rested," said Vanslen.

Rin was then shown to his quarters. The room had a canopy covered bed that faced a wall of complete glass. It was dark now, so there was no view to enjoy, but Rin was curious to see what it would look like come morning. More pillows were scattered about the room and a black stove glowed orange with embers heating the space, however it was still a bit chilly due to all the windows.

Rin slipped into a beautiful lilac satin robe and then got into bed, pulling the heavy blankets up to his nose. He then drifted off into the most peaceful sleep he had in ages. Whether this was from pure exhaustion or the magic surrounding the space was unclear, but the sweet relief of unconsciousness overcame him almost instantly.

Before he could stop himself, Aarush was back in the core. Acting brashly as usual, he was ready to trade the branch for passage to the Winter Kingdom without much planning. Knocking on Soldren's door, he could hardly contain his excitement.

"Back so soon?"

"I have what you want. A branch with berries from the Winter Kingdom."

"Impressive, with this exchange I am happy to get you one round trip passage to and from the Winter Kingdom. Here, take this pendant. Use it to summon me when you want to return," said Soldren, giving Aarush a strange golden pendant with a pattern that looked kind of like a shell.

Soldren and Aarush made their way back to the stone pillars at the center of the core. Soldren sat and meditated calmly. The weather began to change. It got cold, and the sky clouded over. Snow began to fall. The trees which appeared to be in autumn moments ago dropped their leaves, and frost covered their branches. Then, a portal between two different pillars opened. It was the entrance to the Winter Kingdom.

Having felt confident so far, Aarush was a bit surprised that he felt a bit of apprehension about crossing through the portal, but it was the moment he had finally been waiting for. He brushed aside his reservations and took a deep breath and then stepped through the portal. Once through, it sealed off. Aarush couldn't believe it. He was actually standing in the Winter Kingdom. He had entered into some sort of forest. The trees were frosty and had red berries just like the branch he had given Soldren, except these trees were full and beautiful. Snow crunched beneath his feet and flakes danced about in the air. It was night.

After taking in the surroundings Aarush noticed how cold it was. He was dressed for the Summer Kingdom and had not taken into account how cold it would actually be. His short-sleeved shirt, thin pants, and sandaled feet were not effective against the frigid weather. The wind was so cold it cut right through him, and the snowflakes each felt like microscopic needles all over his skin. He immediately began looking for a village where he could take refuge. After trudging through the snow for a bit his feet became so cold, he couldn't feel them, his hands ached, and his body shivered uncontrollably. Thankfully up ahead he saw some lanterns glowing from a small settlement nestled into the side of a mountain.

Entering an inn, Aarush immediately felt better as the heat from a stove warmed the space.

"Traveler, good heavens! Why are you dressed in such clothes?" asked an older woman working at the front desk. "This will never do, come with me and we will get you back on track."

The old woman turned out to be named Zenitha. Rather than questioning Aarush's strange appearance she whisked him off immediately and doted on him like a grandmother to her own grandson. Aarush was pleasantly surprised by this show of kindness.

"My dear boy, you can't go wandering around in such thin clothing. You'll freeze to death. Here, this will do you good," she said pulling a thick cloak out of a large wooden armoire. "What brings you here anyway? You certainly aren't from the Winter Kingdom."

"I'm from the Spring Kingdom," Aarush lied. "I've come hoping to see Rin."

"That'll be no easy task, the queen keeps him under lock and key. Even those of us from here rarely see him except for at parades or royal speeches. There is, however, a banquet coming up, mostly for royalty or predominant community members, but if you could find your way in, I am sure you could meet with him."

After a hearty warm meal of hot soup and cooked vegetables from the nearby mountains, Aarush snuggled into his bed for the night. He was very grateful for the extra blanket Zenitha had given him. His body was not used to the cold at all. He then drifted off to sleep.

That night in his dreams he saw beautiful snowy mountains and then Rin in a lavender colored room sleeping peacefully. He tried calling out to him, but his voice made no sound. He tried everything he could to wake the sleeping prince, but the harder he tried the more the dream faded until he found himself waking up in the guestroom of the inn.

It was morning now and the bed was very cozy and warm. He could hardly motivate himself to brace the cold outside the covers, but one thought of Rin and he bolted out of bed quickly throwing on the heavier clothes and cloak Zenitha had given him.

Down in the kitchen Zenitha had already prepped a hearty breakfast for him consisting of eggs, bread, and jam made from the winter berries. There was also some kind of bitter tea.

"So, how should I go about getting into this banquet you mentioned?" Aarush asked, wasting no time.

"You certainly aren't the most patient," smiled Zenitha, putting more bread on his plate. "There are always limited tickets available for general community members to attend. I am sure they are all sold out by now, but in the main city Xanslo, I have a friend who told me he still had an extra ticket. Go to the market and ask for Vivey."

"I must be going then," Aarush said standing.

"Calm down, if you are meant to be there you will go. Now finish your breakfast so you have strength for the journey."

Aarush sulkily finished his breakfast, but he knew Zenitha was right. He needed as much strength as possible to complete the journey in the cold. After finishing his meal, Aarush paid Zenitha in Winter Kingdom currency, which he had stolen from the Summer Castle treasury before he left. He added on a generous tip as well.

"Dear, I can't accept this much, you'll need it when you get to Xanslo," but after he insisted, she accepted the gift.

"Thank you for letting me borrow your reindeer as well," Aarush said, climbing onto the back of the reindeer. Zenitha had also packed him some food and two bottles of hot bitter tea for the journey. She said it would take one day's time.

"Safe travels," Zenitha wished with a smile.

Aarush was touched by Zenitha's kindness. She was the first person, other than Edna, who seemed to really listen and want to help him.

Rin awoke to the sunrise through the windows in front of his bed. He was quite warm thanks to the thick blankets, but the stove had since been extinguished and his nose, the only thing not covered, was quite cold.

Getting out of bed, Rin admired his quarters in a new light. The window was composed of long, tall panes put together to create one large panoramic view. Each pane was outlined in brass. Due to this design the room was quite cold, and he could feel the air seeping in along the junctions of the panes when he placed his hand on them.

The walls of the room were a dusty lilac and had mirrors of various shapes and sizes hung about like artwork. They made the room feel even bigger. Rin pulled out his cloak and other clothing from the closet and got dressed. Today was the day he could finally enter the library. He wasn't sure what they would find but prayed it would be helpful.

Making his way into the main room Rin was reunited with the other sorceresses who had prepared a traditional Winter Kingdom breakfast which consisted of winter berry tea, steamed vegetables mixed with mushrooms from the mountains, and eggs with bread.

"Rin, good morning. Please join us to eat. You have a long day ahead of you in the library and will need the strength," said Vanslen.

After breakfast Vanslen lead Rin to a different part of the high council's lair. They walked through a breezeway that connected two different parts of the mountain peak. Rin glanced over the edge down into the misty abyss as they crossed. On the opposite side was the library.

"Here we are, all the lore from since the Winter Kingdom began," boasted Vanslen.

Past a heavy wooden door secured by a lock and skeleton key was a vast library that occupied an entire cavern inside the mountain. There were a few small windows, but the space was mostly illuminated by blue glowing mushrooms and strange luminescent pink vines with glittering flowers that draped overhead.

The books, which were mostly large volumes with tattered yellowing pages, sat stacked on bookshelves that reached up to the ceiling. Some shelves even had rolling ladders to reach the upper levels. One strange thing Rin noticed right away was that unlike the palace library which smelled a bit like musty paper, this collection didn't smell musty at all. The dry mountain air must have preserved the books well over time, that or magic.

"Where do we even start?" asked Rin, gazing at the vast stacks of books.

"There is a section for the royalty," said Vanslen, guiding them through the library.

When arriving at the set of bookcases dedicated to royalty Rin was again shocked to find that none of them were labeled. All of the books were a sort of dusty gray color with gold embellishments on the spine, but not a word to denote what was in each volume.

"Is there some kind of catalogue or key to find the topics of these books?" Rin asked.

Vanslen smiled in her knowing way. "You must use your feelings. Reach out. Guide your hand along the books and you will know which one you need."

Rin did as he was told and glided his hand along the books even though it felt like a rather odd way to find the right one. It was such a strange library. Even after gliding his hand over all the volumes, he felt no sort of sensation that told him which book to choose. Pulling one at random he found the pages empty.

"You need to reach out with your heart," smiled Vanslen. "If you don't believe that it will work, it won't."

Trying again, this time Rin closed his eyes and focused on his feelings, something he didn't often do. At first there was nothing, but as he glided his hand over the spines of the books, he suddenly felt a sort of force. Something like a magnet pulling him toward a specific area. He slowly worked his way over to where the sensation was the strongest and suddenly stopped. His hand rested on one of the books and a sensation of warmth spread through his body.

Pulling the book off the shelf, he was delighted to find that it was full of words this time. Perhaps this would yield some answers. Inside he found a diagram of the core. Each kingdom surrounded it, but something was wrong. Flames from the Summer Kingdom leapt though the center and spilled into the Winter Kingdom.

"Vanslen," Rin said nervously as he eyed the diagram, "what do you make of this?"

Vanslen took the book into her withered hands and pondered the strange image before them.

"We should not act in haste, for the prophecies in these volumes are often vague and nuanced. That being said, I think this reaffirms the threat to your life coming from the Summer Kingdom."

"As I told my mother, I have no interest in the Summer Kingdom, nor any connection to it. What is the reason for this attack?"

"My dear, you might not have an interest in the Summer Kingdom, but it seems to have an interest in you," replied Vanslen. "I suggest you get back to the palace. I was told you have a banquet this evening, and it is also safer for you to be in the protection of the palace if there is some threat coming from the Summer Kingdom."

Rin pondered this for a moment. It seemed strange that going back to the palace would be safer. The mountains were so remote, and the sorceress society was very secluded. "Wouldn't it be safer for me to remain here where they can't find me?"

"Perhaps, but it is better for you to keep this place as a last resort of escape rather than a permanent hiding place. Very few know how to find us. You must be strong, after all you are going to be our new leader. You must show the people they can trust you even in times of need."

It hit Rin at that moment that becoming king held far more responsibility than he'd originally imagined.

Vanslen along with a few of the other sorceresses helped load up a sled with the necessities and gifts for the journey back to the palace. The sun from earlier in the day had disappeared behind a thick layer of clouds.

"Better hurry back, Zeb, a storm is brewing," said Vanslen patting the reindeer on the head. He gave a huff of acknowledgement and after saying goodbye to the sorceresses the two sped back off down the mountain. It seemed that whenever they went to the mountains they were always caught in a storm. Rin wondered if perhaps the storms were intentionally created by the sorceresses to mask their travel from prying eyes, but it still made the trips rather difficult.

This storm, however, was different from the others. As they descended the mountain the snow didn't let up, and even when they were onto the plains, flurries brushed by so fast that Zeb would spook and nearly topple the sled.

"Easy now, Zeb, it's just a snowstorm. You have been through plenty of these before," Rin reassured, but inside he knew as clearly as Zeb that the storm was unnaturally strong. He glanced up at the dark clouds as an uneasy feeling grew inside him. Just as they came over a drift a gust of wind so strong lifted them both into the air. The sled spun and Rin couldn't track which way was up or down. The next thing he knew, he saw trees rapidly approaching and then his vision went dark.

AARUSH - RESCUE MISSION

The journey to Xanslo was rather uneventful, but Aarush was in awe of everything he saw along the way. The misty snow-capped mountains in the distance, the crunch of ice under the reindeer's feet, the small cottages nestled into snowdrifts along the trail all captivated him as they trudged onward.

At midday he stopped in a small clearing to have the lunch that Zenitha had packed him. It consisted of bread, berries, and cooked fish. Aarush remembered that he had read that ice fishing was common in the Winter Kingdom while he was doing his research. He was still surprised at how much smaller the portions were in comparison to what he usually ate, but he was still thankful for the meal.

As he and the reindeer continued on, the sky clouded over, and it became much colder. Aarush fished out the extra coat Zenitha had packed in his bag and wrapped a scarf around his neck. Thankfully they were passing through the forest which broke the wind. It whispered through the tall pine trees as their branches danced about with the gusts.

Upon coming to the edge of the clearing onto the plains it was obvious that the storm was getting worse. It was almost impossible to see, and Aarush was considering setting up camp to wait for the storm to pass, hopefully it would only be a few hours and he could still make it to the banquet. He and the reindeer sat at the edge of the forest shielded by some rocks. As they waited, the wind grew even stronger.

Hearing a loud crash, Aarush turned in shock to see an entire sled wedged into the trees. Its reindeer had come unhitched and frantically ran about while the contents of the vehicle were strewn across the forest floor. The passenger lay unconscious on the ground.

Aarush dashed over to the passenger. They didn't stir as he approached, but after a light shake, they sat up groggily. Helping the stranger support himself Aarush knelt down next to them.

"You took quite a spill. Some weather we are having. Are you alright?"

The man turned his head and unwrapped his scarf to reveal his face. Aarush froze. It was Rin. His almond shaped eyes were dark and severe, his straight jet-black hair peeked out around his fur hood, and his clear skin and thin stature, even when bundled up, made him look like a doll sitting in the snow.

It was Rin, Aarush couldn't get any other words out as he stared at him, his heart starting to beat faster.

"Thank you for your help," Rin said, standing up and dusting himself off rather matter-of -factly. "How will I ever get to the banquet on time now."

Aarush saw his chance to get even closer to Rin. "I can give you a ride. My reindeer and I took shelter here before the storm got really bad."

"Your kindness will be rewarded by myself and the queen," said Rin.

Aarush politely declined any monetary compensation. Rin seemed perplexed by his refusal, but he didn't protest. The two then proceeded to pick up the scattered boxes from the overturned sled.

"Here, we can use these blankets to secure the goods on the backs of the reindeer. Too bad your sled is no longer operational," Aarush motioned to the pile of splintered boards and warped metal. Rin nodded, but he didn't seem overly alarmed at the loss of his vehicle.

As the two worked, Aarush continued to steal glances at Rin. Everything about him was so elegant right down to the way he gently picked up the boxes off the forest floor. Hardly a task that the average person could make appear to be a whimsical performance. The most bewitching part of it all was that Rin appeared to have no idea how beautiful he was. The two reindeer had calmed down and stood waiting with the makeshift packs draped over their backs.

"There we go, all loaded up," said Aarush securing the last box. He looked to Rin standing next to his reindeer which was completely white save for its nose, hooves, and antlers which were a light brown. The reindeer Aarush had been lent was a grey brown and appeared to be a bit older than Rin's. Although Rin's reindeer was younger it still was over twice his size and from what Aarush could tell there was no way Rin was going to be able to jump up onto its back.

"Shall we get going?" asked Rin.

"Sure, might I assist you onto your reindeer?" smiled Aarush, secretly excited to show off his strength, especially in front of Rin rather than a group of hunters. This was his moment to shine.

Rin sighed in relief. If it were not for this kind man, he certainly would not have had a way to the banquet. He gratefully agreed to his help getting onto Zeb's back, since he had no saddle with holsters. The man, being much taller than Rin, gently hoisted him onto Zeb without any effort at all. His hands sat on Rin's waist situating him into the correct riding position.

Rin felt a jolt of heat go through his body; it was something he had never felt before. The sensation was so strong he became a bit dizzy, but the second the man removed his hands, the sensation faded away, leaving just a warm feeling that situated itself in Rin's chest.

"Might I ask your name and where you are from?" Rin probed, sensing that this was not an ordinary citizen of the Winter Kingdom.

"Oh, just two towns over. The name is…" the man paused, "Aster."

"Well, I am sure glad you were here, Aster. I fear things would have turned out much differently if I were alone."

"It is a pleasure to help the future king," Aster replied.

Rin thought for a moment. If the man knew who he was he was probably from the Winter Kingdom. Yet his looks were nothing like anyone he had ever seen before, even those from the Spring and Fall Kingdoms didn't compare.

"So, I heard there is a banquet this evening, I assume you are headed there?" asked Aster.

"Indeed, I am," Rin replied. "Will you be accompanying me the duration of the journey?"

"But of course, I am headed there myself," Aster grinned as the two trotted along.

Thankfully the weather had started to improve. While it was still heavily snowing the wind had died down considerably and the Winter Palace could faintly be seen on the horizon. Aarush had so many questions he wanted to ask Rin but decided to save them as to not blow his cover.

Arriving at the palace, the two entered through the foyer for royals and distinguished guests as to avoid the hordes of people who had arrived for the festivities.

"This is Aster, thanks to him I arrived here in one piece. See to it that he is taken care of. The handmaidens can help get him ready. I fear most of our supplies were lost or damaged in the woods."

The guards nodded in acknowledgement. One rang a small bell made of ice that trilled lightly in the snowy breeze. Within moments a group of handmaidens all clad in white dresses with sheer sparkling accents appeared and whisked away Aster.

Juniper accompanied by a few other of Rin's personal handmaidens in mauve dresses joined him.

"What took you so long? The queen has been worried sick."

"A little trouble with the storm on the way back," Rin replied.

"Well, you better be ready for a scolding."

The group made their way to Rin's quarters where they had prepared his coronation garments. A thick white cape, lavender coat, and silver scepter. The crown was in his mother's possession to be bestowed upon him that evening.

Rin looked at his reflection in the mirror. He looked a little worse for wear. Cheek bones slightly sunken in, dark circles under his eyes, and a general air of exhaustion completed his look.

"The outfit is wonderful, but I don't look so good," Rin sighed, glancing over to Juniper.

"It's fine, most people won't be sitting close enough to the royal banquet table to even notice," she replied doing her best to assuage Rin's fears.

Another handmaiden quickly powdered his face which helped a bit.

"There you are. I know you like to run off to the mountains these days, but I can't have you scarcely returning in time for your royal duties. You have to make a good impression to the start of your tenure as King," Anseia burst into the room, her extravagant dress billowing behind her as her handmaidens did their best to tame the fabric.

"I was planning to come back on time. This storm altered my plans. One of the locals, Aster, helped me get here. My sled was damaged. Thankfully I'm not injured."

"Where is this 'Aster' you speak of?"

"The handmaidens are getting him ready. I made sure he is cared for in return for his generosity."

"Good, at least you have done something right today," Anseia sighed.

Despite his mother's scolding, Rin couldn't seem to shake Aster from his mind, especially the moment when he helped place him onto Zeb. That strange jolt of heat though his body. What was it?

AARUSH - A WARM WELCOME IN AN ICY REALM

After arriving at the palace, a group of handmaidens ushered Aarush off before he could even get in another word to Rin. Glancing over his shoulder, he watched as Rin was swept away in the opposite direction. Just when he thought he was getting closer, they had been separated yet again. As much as Aarush wanted to chase after him, it would have created too much of a scene.

Apparently, his outfit was not adequate for the banquet as the handmaidens fussed over which garments they should use to replace his current attire. One came over and trimmed up his hair while another applied shaving cream and smoothed out his face. It was hard to keep track of everything that was being done to his form, but by the end he had been plucked, perfumed, and adorned in an extravagant white and gold outfit with fur lining that showed on the edges of the collar and sleeves.

"Thank you," was all he could manage to the group of women who had single handedly transformed him into a much more handsome version of himself.

The handmaidens giggled at his shocked face as he glanced in the mirror. He looked the best he had in years. The Summer Kingdom was certainly not as fastidious about looks. Of course, he had to look fresh for formal events here and there, but nothing to this extent.

After all the preparations he was ushered into a great hall made of tall trees that had branches that intertwined into a sort of ceiling. Glowing vines had been braided into natural chandeliers. Tables sat interspersed throughout the space with pre-set appetizers of bread and berries. Maids ran about filling cups with hot cider.

Aarush was moved to the front of the grand space due to his help bringing Rin back to the palace. At the front was a long table with various court officials, and elevated above that, another table with Rin and Queen Anseia. The festivities started and Aarush did his best to converse with his tablemates who appeared to be well to do townspeople, but he only half listened as most of his attention was focused on Rin.

Rin sat perched next to his mother and chatted effortlessly with those around him as they came by. It seemed Aarush's appearance hadn't had any effect on Rin, although Aarush had hoped that Rin might show some interest in him as well. After the main course of dinner was cleared away the lights in the space dimmed through some sort of magic and all the focus fell to Rin as one of the court royals came to the front.

"Rin has passed all of the trials in the Winter Kingdom and has the support of the people to become our next king. Queen Anseia will now present him with the royal crown."

Queen Anseia reached for the crown, but at that same moment all the lights blew out and a chill filled the air. The doors in the back burst open and glowing streaks streamed through the space.

"Strange of you to have a coronation without the sorceresses," came a booming voice. "Rin is not only part of the Winter Kingdom, but also part of us magic wielders who live in the mountains."

The townspeople cowered at their tables as an older woman glided to the front of the space. The queen looked horrified, and the royal court cleared a path like a parting sea as the woman walked to the front. The only one that remained unphased was Rin.

"People of the Winter Kingdom, there is no need to fear. The sorceresses are not our enemy," said Rin to the audience.

"A wise leader we have for the Winter Kingdom and realm of the sorceresses," the old lady smiled pulling out a glowing crystal on a necklace. "I bestow upon our future ruler the Crystal of Nyre. May he bring peace to us all."

The old woman put the necklace over Rin's head like a medal of honor and then turned to the audience.

"Continue your festivities," she said as she disappeared into a cloud of glittering, pink, smoke.

Murmurs spread though the audience after the lights came back up. No one seemed to know exactly what to say until one of the royal court members spoke up.

"Rin has shown even now that he will be a great leader. Never before have we had the approval of the sorceresses for one of our rulers. Rin will truly bring peace to the Winter Kingdom. Let us crown him king."

The queen recollected herself and held the royal crown over Rin's head. The crown was exquisite. It was made of frosty entangled branches interspersed with red berries and greenery. As the queen set the crown onto Rin's head a dusting of snow fell over his dark hair. Aarush's heart raced again.

After dinner, the handmaidens approached once more.

"The new king invites you to spend the night at the palace," said one of the women.

He was then guided to the guest quarters. Aarush wondered when he could see Rin again, and he even considered asking the handmaiden about possibly visiting him but decided to keep quiet as to not cause any suspicion.

The room was far more grandiose than the one that he had at the inn. The entire space was made of ice. The window overlooked a frozen lake and Aarush wondered if it ever unfroze as he peered over the outdoor scenery. It was dusk now and the sky was a beautiful pink as the storm had cleared. Ornate furniture in the same color scheme sat around the room.

After getting acquainted with the space Aarush passed out into a peaceful sleep, exhausted by the day's events. Deep in the night he awoke to a knocking at his door. It was freezing. His breath made clouds of steam in the air, his nose was numb, and ice crystals had formed on his eyelashes. He had never felt such cold in his life. Slipping back on his warmest garments, he slid out of bed. To his surprise, Rin was standing on the other side of the door.

After the coronation, Rin retreated to his quarters. It was a lot to take in. He had not expected a surprise visit from Vanslen, and this weighed on him a bit. He wondered to himself if he could effectively maintain the peace between the citizens of the Winter Kingdom and the sorceresses…and then there was Aster. The identity of his mysterious savior clouded his mind as he tried to focus on his new duties as king.

Pulling out the Crystal of Nyre, Rin admired it in the palm of his hand. The crystal was octagonal, glowed a light blue, and hung downward from a single gold chain. It was beautiful, but he could also feel it held a great deal of power and magic, what for he did not know. As he sat pondering these events, he felt he needed to see Aster, figure out who exactly he was, and ascertain the reason behind that shocking sensation when they touched.

Sneaking into the hallway, Rin tiptoed down the stairs of the tower ducking behind statutes, curtains, and pillars. Finally, he had made his way to the guest quarters undetected. Taking a deep breath, he knocked on the door of Aarush's room.

"Rin? What are you doing here?"

"We have to keep quiet. If my mother knows I came to meet you… it will raise a lot of questions," Rin said, slipping inside.

Aster didn't seem to mind his intrusion; in fact, he welcomed it.

"I have to know. Who are you? Earlier, when you helped me up onto my reindeer, I had this feeling. A burning jolt of energy sliced through my body. Are you a sorcerer? Why did you help me?" Rin probed; all of his questions came flooding out at once.

"Rin, you are correct…I am actually…the prince of the Summer Kingdom, Aarush. I came here against the rules, to find you, but I was afraid to say anything earlier fearing I would be sent back. Now that we are alone, and…well, you cornered me…this is the truth."

Rin's heart raced. All the pieces fell into place. No wonder Aarush had seemed different when he was posing as Aster. Rin also immediately recognized that Aarush must be the heat, the warmth, the fire he had been warned of.

"You need to leave," said Rin in the most diplomatic tone he could muster.

"Please, let me explain," said Aarush. "Give me tonight to tell you all the details, and I am sure you will understand."

Rin wanted to say no, he wanted to turn down Aarush, but at the same time, if he played his cards right, he might be able to gain knowledge that could save him and his kingdom, and there was something about Aarush. He was so sincere; he didn't really seem like a threat.

"Fine, but we can't talk here," he said, questioning what he was doing. "There is a small palace in the foothills that was used in the past by royals as a vacation home. It is abandoned now, but it is the perfect place to get away from everything, and it is the last place anyone would look. We can spend the night there which will give you plenty of time to explain, and you can drop me back at the main palace before the sun rises."

The two princes slipped out of the room with Rin leading the way. As they approached the foyer, Rin turned to Aarush.

"This part is going to be tricky. There are many guards."

"I could create a diversion," offered Aarush, pointing to a vine tied to the wall. It was holding up a chandelier above the space.

Before Rin stop him, Aarush had released the rope, and the chandelier came crashing down into the foyer. In the smoke from the extinguished candles the two bolted out of the space and made their way to the reindeer barn.

With Aarush's help it took no time to hitch Zeb to a sleigh. The next thing Rin knew they were flying across the moonlight snow. He couldn't help but gaze at Aarush. Thankfully Zeb knew the way their destination, so he didn't have to keep his eyes ahead of them. Aarush seemed equally interested. They had locked eyes, and Rin marveled at Aarush's sculpture like features in the moonlight., Aarush leaned over trying to put his arm around Rin's shoulders. Rin quickly scooted over in the seat.

"I…I think I need to keep my eyes on the road," Rin said, his heart pounding in his chest.

Aarush looked at him sheepishly. From the expression on his face, Rin couldn't tell if he was embarrassed or simply regretful at failing to make a move. In that moment, Rin felt pulled in two directions. A part of him wanted nothing more than to drop Aarush on the side of the road and move on as if nothing ever happened, but something in his heart seemed to have melted a bit. Although at first he worried Aarush was the dangerous heat he had heard in the prophecies and warnings, he wondered if Aarush was actually sent to help him stop or prevent a greater danger. Rin decided that it might be okay to let down his guard ever so slightly.

Zeb pulled up to the second palace. Purple flowers poked through the snow in bunches around their feet and tall fir trees surrounded the space, completely shielding it from the view of anyone on foot.

The palace itself was small, one might not even call it a palace at all save for the spires that surrounded the more geometric parts of the building. A fresh snow covered the peaks of the spires and ornate eves of the structure. The entire edifice was constructed of a white stone interspersed with stained glass windows.

Aarush removed his cloak, wrapping it around Rin's shoulders as the two disembarked from the sleigh and walked toward the palace entrance. Rin smiled to himself in amusement, Aarush was certainly less adapted to the cold, but he appreciated the gesture.

Once inside the palace their footsteps echoed in the main foyer. It was dark, and the only light that entered was from the moon refracting though the stained glass windows. Rin guided them silently through the labyrinth of hallways to the bedchambers.

Aarush started a fire in the fireplace and the two sat on the bed thankful for the heat.

"So, tell me everything," said Rin.

Aarush recounted his story, and to Rin's surprise, there did not seem to be any intent to take his life or attack his kingdom, and the urgency and sincerity with which Aarush spoke made Rin wonder if perhaps Aarush wasn't the threat he originally assumed him to be.

"Aarush, you must know that there is a prophecy that an attack on my life, and this realm, will come from the Summer Kingdom."

Aarush's eyes widened. "Rin, I will help you however I can to prevent this threat. You have my word. Upon my return, I will immediately send out my army to search for whatever might be the cause."

Rin felt a weight lift off his shoulders. Perhaps Aarush was here to help, maybe the sprites had somehow intervened to give him a chance at stopping the attack from the Summer Kingdom before it even began. With this new knowledge Rin let down his guard a bit more, he asked Aarush many questions about the Summer Kingdom and Aarush asked many in turn about the Winter Kingdom as well. The two talked late and dozed off as the fire they had started turned to smoldering embers.

That night Rin awoke wrapped in Aarush's strong arms. At first, he tried to push away, but it was no use with Aarush's strength. Giving up, Rin embraced Aarush's warmth; the type of warmth that radiated off Aarush's body was something different than sitting by a fireplace, or stove. It was more intense and almost felt as if it were melting him from the inside out. Rin also noticed his own heart start to flutter.

The next morning, Aarush awoke to Rin sleeping peacefully next to him. It was still early enough that the moon gleamed brightly through the window. The fire was completely extinguished without even a single glowing ember left.

"Time to get up," Aarush gently shook Rin. Rin was most certainly a prince. Even when he slept, his beauty was astounding. Aarush stared at him as he stirred, the moonlight illuminating his porcelain skin. He pushed Rin's bangs out of his face and started to lean in to kiss his forehead when Rin opened his eyes. Aarush pulled back quickly.

At first Rin seemed calm, but as the realization of their questionable rendezvous came back into the forefront of his mind he bolted upright.

"Okay, time to get me back before sunrise. Tonight was…" Rin trailed off, but Aarush could tell that there were no hard feelings.

On their sleighride back to the main palace, Aarush was overcome by the realization that this might be the last time he could see Rin for a while, he wondered if he could extend their time just a bit longer.

"Rin, there are still a few hours until the sun rises, come with me to see the Summer Kingdom."

Aarush could tell by the look on Rin's face that he initially wanted to say no, but before he could form the syllables on his lips Aarush jumped in again.

"Think about it, this is very well your one and only chance. After you become king, it is unlikely we will see each other again and even less likely that you will leave your kingdom."

Rin paused after hearing Aarush's proposal. While earlier he would have definitively said "no," after spending the night with Aarush, and seeing that perhaps Aarush really did want to help him find and extinguish the fire and heat that threatened his life, things were different. Also, his feelings for Aarush had started to grow, realizing this might be the last time he ever spent with him, visiting the Summer Kingdom was an enticing proposal. This could function as the closure to whatever feelings they had both developed. Taking a deep breath Rin made his decision.

"I want to see it. I want to see the Summer Kingdom."

Rin watched as Aarush smiled and pulled a pendant out of his cloak. It glowed and a portal opened, and they dashed through into… the core.

Rin had studied the core when becoming a royal, but he had never been given the chance to visit due to his mother's concern of him leaving the kingdom. It was beautiful. Every season at once and somehow no season at all. He breathed in the warmer air and felt his spirits lift. Even if this was a poor decision, he would be bound to the rules of being king the rest of his life, what was a couple hours away to see the world. It would be okay…he reassured himself.

"Soldren. I'm back," said Aarush.

"I see you have company," said Soldren. "First time I've seen royals cross to the opposite season. Best of luck to the two of you…you'll need it."

Opening another portal back to the Summer Kingdom Rin felt the hot, humid air brush over his skin. The Summer Kingdom was something to behold. Green trees stretched as far as the eye could see. The sky was a clear blue, and a waterfall could be seen in the distance.

"I have never seen this much green in my life," Rin smiled in spite of himself.

"I'm glad I could show it to you. We deserve to see each other's kingdoms. I found the Winter Kingdom just as awe inspiring as you find it here."

Aarush put a hand onto Rin's back. Again, Rin felt the heat pass through his being. Pulling away, Rin smiled.

"Thank you for this. I have followed the rules all my life. I didn't realize how free I could feel." It felt like a weight had been lifted off of his shoulders, he wanted to run through the lush grass, splash in a waterfall, anything he could in this finite moment of pure freedom before he had to return to his ordinary life.

The two hitched Zeb to a nearby tree and made their way to the Summer Kingdom's castle. Aarush led them in through a secret passageway to his quarters where Rin could change into some more appropriate clothing. Aarush handed Rin a brown tunic and pants. Rin was surprised at the lightness of the material compared to what he wore in the Winter Kingdom. The fabric seemed to float on his body.

"I have something I want to show you," smiled Aarush.

Rin followed along to a barn full of beautiful, red birds.

"This is Signo," said Aarush patting one of the birds on the side. "He and I have hunted together since I was a boy. Take a ride with us."

Not knowing what to expect, Rin jumped on the back of the bird with the help of Aarush again. Once on the bird Aarush grabbed his hands, placing them around his waist. Rin smiled toward him, carefree in this new kingdom. With his newfound trust in Aarush Rin felt himself...dare he say, growing fond of their relationship.

"Hold on," he smiled back at Rin. Their faces were inches apart.

Rin's heart fluttered once more. He held tight onto Aarush as they soared into the sky. The warmth grew inside him, but this time instead of fighting against it, Rin let it melt a bit of himself. There was something alluring about the heat.

They flew higher and higher until they were right above the surface of the sun. The heat was almost scorching, but Rin wanted to see more. As they glided above the surface, fish unlike any he had ever seen before jumped about.

Swinging Signo around, Aarush started to have the trio descend back toward the Summer Kingdom. Then Rin saw it. All the kingdoms from above. The Summer Kingdom was green with mountaintops covered in a light mist. Fall was clear with many red, gold, and orange trees dotting the landscape. Spring was full of flowers of all colors, and Winter was a solid white due to the clouds.

Rin lost his breath. It was one of the most beautiful things he had ever seen. At that moment Aarush turned back to him, his smile wide. Before Rin knew what was happening, their lips touched in a kiss.

Rin wasn't entirely sure if he was doing anything correctly. Was this how one was supposed to kiss? He had never had a romantic relationship in his life. What if Aarush thought he was awkward? All these thoughts melted away as Aarush held him closer. Rin felt heat shoot through his body and was happier than he had ever been before, but after the initial rush he felt a pain in his chest. A sort of breaking…shattering happened within him. The world started to fade, and the last thing he saw was the bright surface of the sun.

AARUSH - DISASTER

Aarush looked back at Rin to see his reaction to the realms below them. Rin's dark black hair was blown to the side from the flight revealing his violet eyes, his lips a rose against his porcelain skin. Aarush couldn't contain himself anymore. He leaned in for a kiss and to his surprise Rin leaned in too. As their lips touched, Aarush felt a cold penetrate his body. It seeped into his core and spread throughout his limbs. It was almost painful. As he pulled away from the kiss, Rin passed out in his arms.

"Rin? Rin! Are you okay?" Aarush cradled Rin. He truly looked and felt like a doll, something lifeless. Aarush felt his stomach turn and his heart seemed to freeze in panic.

The only sign that Rin was still alive was the slight rise and fall of his chest. Aarush and Signo sped back to the forest near the palace where he laid Rin on the ground in a meadow flooded with sunshine hoping to warm up his cold body. Signo wrapped himself around them for even more warmth. The flowers and grass around Rin's body became frosted as he lay in the sun, causing everything around them to sparkle.

"Come on Rin," whispered Aarush, cradling Rin's head in his lap.

His plan had almost been perfect, but now he couldn't think of what to do. If he called a palace medic, it would expose that he'd brought royalty from the opposite kingdom into their realm. As he sat fretting over what to do, a strong rushing sound could be heard in the distance.

Aarush didn't even notice until a small stream of water touched his leg that the rushing was water. He glanced up in time to see a large wave crashing through the forest. Trees toppled as the wave grew closer and closer. Grabbing Rin, Aarush jumped onto Signo and flew up into the air as the top of the wave spewed mist onto the trio as they glided above the flood below.

As they soared higher, Aarush could see that the flood had covered a large portion of the Kingdom. He felt a sinking feeling in his stomach. He was probably to blame for the catastrophe. There wasn't time to think about this; he had to figure out how to save Rin. Hopefully saving Rin would also restore balance.

Signo soared up to the cliff where they had tethered Zeb. Thankfully the reindeer was unharmed, although a bit startled. The only thing that came to mind was getting to Soldren to get Rin back to the Winter Kingdom. Aarush once again pulled out the medallion he had been gifted and opened the portal to the core. Aarush, Rin, Signo, and Zeb entered the realm as the portal sealed behind them. Strangely, the core was unaffected by the weather in the Summer Kingdom. In the core, all the seasons blended harmoniously as usual.

Soldren came running from his cabin into the clearing.

"What are you doing back here? My goodness, what has become of Rin?!"

"I…" Aarush looked away in shame. "I kissed him."

"Goodness, did you not learn anything about the tragedies that can occur with love across the realms?" asked Soldren, worried wrinkles forming on his forehead.

"I did, but in the moment…I forgot it all."

Soldren shook his head and stayed silent for a moment.

"Well, no use scolding you, what has been done is finished," he said finally. "Now you are seeking to bring Rin back to the Winter Kingdom. Am I correct?"

"Yes, please. I will do whatever is needed to get him back."

"What do you have to trade?"

"Excuse me?" Aarush's eyes widened.

"You heard me, what do you have to trade?"

"I don't have anything to trade you. Is there any way you can make an exception? I don't know how much time Rin has left."

"Sorry, but unless you have something to trade, there is nothing I can do to help you."

"You are nothing more than a crook," Aarush shouted at Soldren.

"No, just business," the old man replied.

Aarush glared back. He had mistaken Soldren's greed for kindness. The man had no empathy whatsoever. All business even when someone's life was on the line.

"If you want to do business, you can leave. I will save Rin with or without you. Once this is over, I will not let your lack of kindness go unpunished," Aarush fumed.

Soldren shrugged and sauntered back down the path to his cabin as if he had not a care in the world.

Turning his attention back to Rin, Aarush was at a loss for what to do. Signo sat on his one side and Zeb on his other. Zeb huffed, although Aarush was unable to tell what he was trying to say. In his exasperation he began to cry, something he rarely did. Once he started, though, the tears wouldn't stop. As he cried, he didn't see his tears spill over Rin's crystal necklace.

The crystal glowed brightly and in a misty cloud the old woman from the banquet appeared with two other younger sorceresses beside her.

"Why did you summon us, young one?" said the older woman in a caring tone.

"Who are you?" Aarush jumped back in shock.

"I'm Vanslen, the leader of the sorceresses. We foresaw that you would call us and that Rin would be in danger, but it was too late to stop you."

"I'm sorry, we just…"

"Love does strange things, dear," Vanslen said.

"You are not angry with me?"

"Of course not. This event was forecasted for years, although we didn't know exactly what would happen. You and Rin's fates have been intertwined since the moment you were born. That is not something you can easily change. What is important is that we work to get Rin back where we can cure him."

"Soldren won't help us. We are stuck here in the core."

"Soldren…ha…how is that old swindler? What he didn't tell you is that he is not the only one with power to traverse between the Kingdoms. There are other ways. I'll gather the other sorceresses."

Vanslen then rang a bell and other sorceresses came into view in the mist. They began to chant, and the mist grew more and more dense. As the light was closing out, Aarush heard Soldren yelling in protest, but it was too late to stop them. The sorceresses had transported them back into the Winter Kingdom.

The group found themselves in a rather familiar room. Aarush realized it was the room he had the vision of Rin in when he first entered the Winter Kingdom. Rin lay covered in velvet purple blankets in an ornate bed in what Aarush guessed was the lair of the sorceresses in the mountains.

"Stay back, please." Vanslen gestured to Aarush, Signo, and Zeb to move aside as she walked through with a group of sorceresses. They gathered around Rin and continued to chant. The day grew later and later. As the sun began to set Aarush walked to the window to look out. He stood in shock. The trees on the snowy mountainsides had bloomed with pink blossoms. His actions had wreaked havoc in the Winter Kingdom too.

The chanting continued late into the night by firelight. Rin didn't seem to be improving according to a young sorceress. By morning the chanting had died down to a low murmur.

"We cannot save him this way," sighed Vanslen clearly defeated. "He will have to be frozen until a greater magic can save him."

Aarush looked at her pleadingly. "You can't save him? What is more powerful than magic? Would love work? Although we just met, I have developed feelings for Rin, perhaps this could help save him."

"Dear, love is what caused the harm in this case. Love isn't always a cure. Sometimes it is a poison. Your warmth partially melted his heart. If his heart fully thaws, he will perish."

Aarush slumped into his seat. The next hours brought him more pain than he thought possible. The sorceresses performed a ritual to fully freeze Rin to keep his heart from completely melting. After the ritual was completed Rin's body was fully covered in a thin layer of frost. His skin looked even paler than usual, and his rosy lips were now more of a pale pink. His beautiful eyes closed.

"You must go before his mother comes," advised Vanslen. "She will not be as understanding as we are. Here, take these gifts to Soldren. He will grant you asylum in the core for now, as I assume you can't return to the Summer Kingdom immediately."

And with that, Aarush gave a pat to Zeb and left with Signo through a portal back to the core. He glanced back over his shoulder at Rin's sleeping, frozen body. A tear slid down his cheek.

Shaking my head, I found myself back in my grandmother's living room as usual. I was sitting next to her on the velvety purple sectional, and while the stove had died down a bit, the pot of glogg still had wisps of steam emanating off of it. Nothing was amiss as if the wonderful story never took place.

"What happened to Rin and Aarush then?"

"Aarush continues hiding in the core to this day to avoid being severely punished. Whenever his anger about his failure with Rin boils, the summer gets unusually hot. Rin remains frozen in ice. He gets colder each year and winter becomes more and more harsh, as you can see from the storm tonight."

"It doesn't seem fair that two people that loved each other so much would end up living eternally in pain."

"Life isn't fair, Mikael," my grandmother gave me a pat on the shoulder. "There is a shrine dedicated to each of the Seasonal Kingdoms in the mountains near here. Perhaps going there will help you feel better. Why don't you go tomorrow when the weather clears up?"

That night, I couldn't sleep. As the wind howled through the trees outside, I couldn't get my mind off of Rin and Aarush. Two people with their fates already determined to work against them. It just didn't make sense. And wasn't love usually the solution in fairy tales, not the problem? I had fully expected my grandmother's story to end with a kiss saving the couple rather than tearing them apart. I finally was able to drift off after tossing about with my thoughts.

The next day the weather was slightly better. It was still heavily snowing, but the wind was gone. Big snowflakes drifted about outside the bedroom window. I swung my legs out of bed and slid my feet into some fur lined slippers, the only thing warm enough to block out the mountain cold. Wrapping the quilt around my shoulders, I shuffled out to the kitchen where my grandmother was already preparing breakfast.

The kitchen of the house was another one of my favorite places. It had white and yellow striped wallpaper that was interspersed with pink roses. Well-loved-cream-colored cabinets hung on the other parts of the walls. An old-fashioned wood stove warmed the space from the corner. A pendant light overhead gave off a warm glow. The kitchen table had a pink and white checkered cloth and was set with two plates. In the center near the window sat a vase of flowers, how they remained alive was beyond me. The window framed the table and looked out over the snowy mountains. The cabin was nestled in a grove of pine above a valley so there wasn't much space outside the window before a sharp cliff like grade into the snow dusted hollow below.

"I see you're up," smiled my grandmother, bringing over fresh waffles as I sat down at the table.

My mother would not have permitted me to remain wrapped in the quilt at the table, but my grandmother didn't seem to mind as the cabin was chilly in the morning despite both stoves being filled with crackling embers.

"So, are you headed to the shrine today?"
I nodded.

"Good, I'll pack you lunch to take along as well as a few things you can put as an offering for each season. I think you will really like it up there. I often go myself when I just want to get away from everything."

After breakfast, I bundled myself up and took the picnic basket that my grandmother had prepared.

"You'll need this," she said, handing me a map.

"Thank you," I replied, looking at the worn paper. It plotted a path from behind the cabin up the side of the mountain to the shrine.

I set out and found that the temperature wasn't as bad as I originally expected. It was peaceful as I trudged up the path through the drifts. I stopped for a moment to look over the mountain range. It was beautiful to see all the snowcapped trees and hear the birds chirping in the breeze. I continued on and got higher and higher. When I was nearly at the tree line, I saw the shrine. The path I was on led to the foot of a precariously steep stone stairway. At the top sat a stone gate with sculptures on both sides.

After shimmying my way up to avoid slipping on the ice I found myself on a sort of platform in front of the shrine which was built into the side of the mountain. A gust of wind blew snowflakes across the entrance. I walked up and found that there were four sculptures…a cherry blossom, flame, leaf, and snowflake. A symbol for each season. I sat down and caught my breath before reaching into the picnic basket.

Inside the basket, which was lined with the same material as the tablecloth in the kitchen, I found my lunch. A simple ham and cheese sandwich and a thermos of hot tea. I ate and warmed up with the tea while feeling a sense of calm I had never felt before. Under my lunch I found what my grandmother had prepared for the offerings. Live cherry blossoms for spring, a candle with matches for summer, fall leaves for autumn, and a snipping of the red berries from the plants in the living room for winter.

I carefully placed each item on the shelves in front of each sculpture.

"If you are there, spirits, please help Rin and Aarush," I said as I lit the candle.

I then sat and watched the alter with all of the offerings. After a while I decided to head back down the mountain as it was starting to get colder, but when I turned to exit though the gate, I found the gate had transformed into a sort of portal. I stared in shock, eyes wide. I must have been freezing to death. I pulled out the thermos and drank some more hot tea, but nothing changed. The shining portal remained in front of me.

Although I was a bit taken aback by the events occurring before my eyes, at the same time I was no stranger to magic as I had experienced my grandmother's lifelike stories. I decided to put my logical thoughts aside and step through.

I knew I had entered the core the second I stepped through the portal. It was just as I saw it during my grandmother's storytelling. In a daze, I followed the trail I remembered to the small cottage, but to my surprise, unlike in the story, there were two cottages. One was definitely Soldren's, but the other was newer and more makeshift, built out of various branches with mud mortar walls and a thatch roof on which moss had grown. A man sat outside whittling a piece of wood.

When he looked up, I recognized him immediately. It was Aarush. I blinked again, wondering if everything around me was real or if I had somehow slipped into another vision during a storytelling session, but unlike during the stories everything felt much more real. I could feel the breeze on my skin, the grass under my boots, and the warmth of the sunshine.

"Aarush?" I managed to get out only his name. It felt strange to meet him in person and not just as an observer of his story.

His head whipped in my direction, and he stood, startled.

"Who are you? How did you find me?"

"I made an offering to the shrine, and it opened a portal to the core."

"What shrine? Which season's kingdom did you come from?"

"I didn't come from any season… I just came from the Svlavian mountains."

Aarush looked at me inquisitively. As he stood pondering, Soldren appeared from his cabin.

"Well, who do we have here?"

"I'm Mikael...of the Svlavian mountains," I said trying to figure out how one might do introductions without being from any season. "I don't come from any of the seasonal kingdoms."

"You are...an outsider?" asked Soldren.

"An outsider?"

"The prophecies of old spoke of an outsider. One without a season who would bring balance." Soldren let out a hearty laugh. "Maybe you'll be the one to finally get Aarush out of my hair."

"How long have you been hiding here?" I asked turning to Aarush.

"It's been years," he replied.

"I'm not sure if I am the one the prophecy speaks of. I came here more or less on accident, not with the intention of restoring any kind of balance."

"Whatever the case, run along, I'll take my chances," Soldren said, beaming.

I couldn't tell if he was happier about the balance or getting the core back to himself again.

"You must go to the Winter Kingdom to save Rin. Frozen in ice all these years, what a horrible way to live...if you can call it that."

"I can't accompany you," Aarush said, turning to me. "I fear what the queen will do to me if I ever show my face in the Winter Kingdom again."

"Aarush, I know your story. As much as you don't want to go to the Winter Kingdom, if I do, I'll need a guide, and to be honest, you need to take responsibility for your actions. Also, I would like to make it clear. Sending me to the Winter Kingdom may not have any affect at all. I didn't come here to bring balance."

"I'm sending you both whether you like it or not," Soldren ushered us along the path as we tried our best to explain that his work could be in vain. "I'll have none of your nonsense. I am willing to gamble a bit."

Once in the center of the core, Soldren opened the portal to the Winter Kingdom, and before we could protest any further, he pushed us through sealing the portal behind us.

"He's as selfish as I had imagined," I said aloud.

"How do you know of him?" asked Aarush.

"My grandmother told me about him," I replied. Thanks to my grandmother's magical stories, I had actually seen Soldren as if he were right in front of me before ever meeting him, but explaining this would have taken too much time.

Thankfully I was bundled up from earlier before entering…wherever we were, but Aarush was not prepared for the cold. I had to chuckle to myself that he was almost in the exact same situation as when he first came to the Winter Kingdom.

"Here, take my scarf and outer coat. I'll be warm enough with the rest of what I have on, plus I have some warm tea we can drink if needed," I said motioning to the picnic basket I was holding. I had nearly forgotten about it until the thought of tea came to mind.

"Thank you," said Aarush shrugging on the coat and wrapping the scarf around his neck. "I never seem to be prepared when I come here."

"In theory you shouldn't be here at all, right?" I asked, already knowing the answer. "Makes sense you wouldn't have the necessary attire."

"Let's see if we can find the inn I stayed at last time. I think I remember the way, and the weather is a lot better this time. Should make travel faster."

We trudged through the snow until we saw the quaint town up ahead. As Aarush remembered there was a small inn. Stepping inside we met Zenitha, who I remembered from my grandmother's story.

"Goodness, you've returned. Still haven't taken to wearing warm clothing I see," she laughed, rubbing Aarush's arm. Then, she glanced over to me. "And you've brought a friend this time. Welcome, it has been so many years. I am glad you are back. I was so worried about you. A palace guard returned my reindeer and I had never heard from you afterward and thought something terrible must have happened."

"I did actually get myself into a bit of a predicament, but I am glad I can see you again," said Aarush.

"And who might you be?" Zenitha asked, turning her attention to me.

"I'm Mikael, nice to meet you."

"You must be from here, you certainly know how to dress warmly," Zenitha chuckled. "Now let's get you two warmed up."

After a lovely warm meal, we found ourselves loaded up onto Zenitha's reindeer, just like in the story. Thankfully, Aarush remembered the way and due to the weather being cooperative we were able to make it to the palace by the end of the day.

The Winter Palace was as beautiful as I remembered from the story, but truly being in front of it was an even more grand. As the sun was setting upon our arrival rosy, pink hues reflected off the ice structure.

"Stop right there. State your name and business," a palace guard said as we approached the gate.

While the palace could clearly be seen from afar, upon closer inspection it was surrounded by a sort of wall made of trees. The gate in front of us was shiny gold. The palace guards wore dark blue velvet cloaks with black helmets that were adorned with painted red winter berries.

Once the guards saw that Aarush was atop the reindeer, they immediately ushered us though without any questions. I wondered why they simply let him in, could it be some sort of trap? I could sense Aarush's body tense up as we dismounted Zenitha's reindeer in the courtyard. We then entered the foyer of the palace accompanied by two guards.

Once inside, a woman in a sparkling white dress floated down the hallway with a few scrolls under her arm.

"Pleased to meet you. I am Ceroa, head attendant to the queen. She requests your presence immediately."

Upon receiving the rather curt welcome, we were quickly guided up a winding spiral staircase. I could only guess that Rin had been moved to the palace after the sorceresses had frozen him. My theory proved correct as we entered Rin's quarters.

"Your majesty," said Aarush, bowing as the queen glided over.

Then before I could comprehend what was happening, the queen deftly slapped Aarush across the face. The sound of the slap reverberated off the walls as everyone around stood in shock.

"I guess I deserved that," Aarush said after a pause.

"You deserve a lot more than that," the queen replied. "To be honest, the only reason I am not having you beheaded is that perhaps you have a way to help us save Rin, since it was you that put him in this position. Although, if you have nothing, we will continue with your punishment. Be glad I am not deciding alone how you will be dealt with. The royal court will decide your fate together. You can beg for mercy when you appear before them."

Aarush, still in a bit of shock, just motioned to me.

"I…" I gulped as the queen stared me down with her striking violet eyes. My legs quivered a bit. "I am the one without a season," I said, remembering what Soldren had mentioned earlier, hoping that bringing it up would be my saving grace. I certainly didn't want to be included in any beheading.

The queen paused, looked me up and down, and while her body remained tense, her eyes softened.

"You are here for Rin, yes?"

"I don't really know why I am here, but if there is something I can do to help Rin, I will."

"Follow me," Anseia replied.

We made our way through Rin's quarters, where we found him lying still. He was strikingly beautiful, even while frozen. His lips were a pale pink. His frosted skin sparkled in the moonlight that came through the window. One might have mistaken him for a sculpture if it were not for the nearly imperceptible cloud of steam that emanated from his nose with each shallow breath.

Aarush reached out to Rin.

"Aarush, stop. You need to be careful," I said, not really knowing what to do.

"Perhaps a kiss would wake him up," offered Aarush.

"Your kiss was what put him here in the first place," I said sternly.

Aarush backed away without any counter argument. I looked at Rin. My heart broke for him. He ended up frozen forever because of how Aarush had carelessly handled their relationship.

In fact, as I stood pondering, I realized that Aarush never had Rin's best interest in mind. Although the story at first seemed like a tale of two forbidden lovers, it really told the tale of a selfish prince who was willing to risk the livelihood of another for the sake of his passion. I knelt next to Rin's bed and held his hand. It was ice cold but not lifeless or stiff.

"Rin, you need to come back for your kingdom. You need to come back and give a second chance. Not to Aarush, not to your mother, but to yourself. Yes, you made a mistake, but you can't give up now. Overcoming this will show the kingdom that you are their true and rightful king."

I didn't know what else to do. I wasn't any sort of wizard and had no command of magic like so many of the beings I was surrounded by. I was torn away from my thoughts by the queen gasping.

"He's unfreezing!"

Sure enough, starting from his hand I was holding, color began to flood back into Rin's skin, his lips became brighter, the frost on his hair turned to dewdrops. He stirred and opened his eyes as he turned to see who had hold of his hand.

"You must be Mikael."

"How do you know who I am?"

"I dreamed of you. I saw you at a shrine in the mountains. I knew you were coming to save me."

"I didn't even know I was coming to save you."

"But you did," Rin smiled as he kept hold of my hand. However, his smile faded as soon as he saw Aarush. "What are you doing here?"

"I brought Mikael. I wanted to save you too. I still love you and I never stopped."

"No, you didn't love him," I disagreed, standing up. "If you loved him, you would have respected his space, talked with the sprites, the royals, or someone to see if you could find a way to be together without harm. While it isn't fair that you can't be with someone from the opposite kingdom, that does not give you the right to recklessly force your way to get what you want. Aarush, you care about your passion, not about Rin."

The room went completely silent. I felt a sort of confidence I had never felt before in my life. I turned to Rin.

"Rin, Aarush was not meant for you, not because he was from the Summer Kingdom, but because he never truly cared about you. He may have had passion for you, but not love. You deserve to find a prince who loves you for who you are, not because you are something they can't have, or see as a challenge." I turned to the others. "The rest of you are not free from error either. The system you have here is unfair, unjust, and is the root of this problem to start with. Anyone from any season should be able to be together."

The room remained silent after I finished. I didn't really know what had come over me. As we stood in silence, glowing streaks filled the air similar to at the banquet.

"Vanslen?" gasped Anseia.

"Grandmother?" I said aloud.

Before me stood my own grandmother. She was dressed just as Vanslen was in the story, wearing a long plum-colored cloak, grey leather boots, and her white hair tied up in a neat bun.

"Yes, Mikael, I masked my image when I told you the story so you wouldn't recognize me, but I am indeed not only your grandmother, but Vanslen as well. That's how I knew you would be the one to bring balance to the kingdoms and Svlavian Mountains."

I stood; eyes wide in shock.

"Anseia, what Mikael said is true. No one party is at fault for what happened here, but the system is flawed. We must contact the sprites to reach a settlement that will benefit all the kingdoms."

My grandmother, or Vanslen, then turned to me.

"You probably have a lot of questions," she said.

Although my grandmother thought I would have questions, everything finally made sense. Her stories, the portal, and this other magical world, they all fit together like a puzzle.

"It is true, I am Vanslen, sorceress of the Winter Kingdom. I also am your grandmother in your realm. I pass between both spaces, a kind of intermediary between the realm of the seasons and the world that they affect. I fell in love in your realm and married your grandfather before his passing. He had no magic abilities and so when I had your mother, she had none either, however something strange happened. You maintained some low level of power yourself."

"You mean I am a sorcerer?"

"In a sense, yes. While you don't have as strong of powers as most sorcerers do, you have the essence of magic within you. This is what gave you the unique ability to bring balance to the seasons. You were able to enter and save Rin with your pure heart and mind. You saw everything from an external perspective, and you also didn't rely on magic to fix your problems. You truly cared."

"But how was that enough to save Rin or bring any kind of balance?"

"You realize, Mikael, that sometimes the kind of love people need isn't romantic. The love of friends and family can be just as powerful if not more so. Sometimes passionate romantic love can be toxic and harmful. The platonic love from friends and family heals. It expects nothing in return and has only the good of the recipient in mind. That love is what you gave Rin."

"Thank you, grandma," I smiled.

While I knew it would still take me much time to process what I had been through and accept the new things I learned about myself and family, I realized my grandmother had given me the same kind of love I gave Rin. She believed in me, nurtured me, and expected nothing in return. The best kind of love one could ever ask for.

As we prepared to leave, I turned to see Rin and Aarush facing each other.

"I think I can find it in my heart to forgive you someday, but for now, please return to your kingdom. You have your duties, and now I can return to mine," said Rin.

"As you wish," Aarush replied with a bow. As tough as he usually appeared, I could see him fighting back the tears welling up in his eyes as the two parted.

Turning toward me, Rin's gaze softened.

"As for you Mikael, I can't express in words how thankful I am for everything you have done. The Winter Kingdom is truly indebted to you. Please come back any time. There will always be a place for you here among our people."

"I think our job here is done." My grandmother smiled putting her hand on my shoulder. "Let's go home."

Streaks of light surrounded us, and Aarush and Rin faded away as the familiar sights of my grandmother's cabin took their palace.

MIKAEL – EPILOGUE

I never disclosed to my family what I knew about my grandmother or what she had told me. Another little secret between the two of us. I came to accept myself and the magic that resided within me. Even though I wasn't really a sorcerer, I felt the magic translated into confidence in the real world. While before I was apprehensive to try new things, or speak my mind, having been through magical realms I felt that now I could take on any challenge.

I continued to visit my grandmother often. On occasion, I would traverse with her into the Winter Kingdom. While the change didn't happen right away, eventually the sprites abolished the rule preventing relationships between opposite seasons. To avoid natural disasters the sprites decided to make the seasons less defined.

Now sometimes there is a strangely warm day in the winter when the snow all but melts or a rather cool day in summer where the rain drizzles and one feels like putting on a light jacket. These days are thanks to lovers from opposite seasons meeting.

Rin went on to become a kind, caring leader who always kept the best interests of his kingdom forefront as he pushed forward to create a fair system for everyone across seasons. He did eventually get married to a prince from the Fall Kingdom. Aarush renounced the right to the throne and became a librarian taking Edna's place when she retired with the aim of helping future leaders avoid the mistakes he made. One of the Summer Kingdom dukes then became next in line for the throne.

While the weather became less predictable in the Svlavian mountains, love became less complicated. In the end love still won, just not the way I would have ever expected in a fairytale.